THE NEW STORY OF O

She took the nipple between her thumb and forefinger, and gradually tightened her grip until she saw the girl's eyes close in pain; and then she pulled, stretching the breast into a perfect cone. As she released the nipple, her other hand swung in a wide arc and delivered a vicious slap to the lower part of the girl's left buttock. Jane neither moved nor cried out.

'Well. Perhaps you are ready, after all . . .'

THE NEW
STORY OF O

NEXUS

A NEXUS BOOK

published by

the Paperback Division of
W. H. Allen & Co. plc

A Nexus Book
Published in 1990
by the Paperback Division of
W H Allen & Co Plc
Sekforde House, 175/9 St John Street
London EC1V 4LL

Typeset by Avocet Robinson, Buckingham
Printed and bound in Great Britain by
Cox & Wyman Ltd, Reading, Berkshire

ISBN 0 352 32494 5

FOREWORD

Following the story that unfolded in *Return to Roissy*, it seemed that O was finished. *I'll be your whore* – Heloise's proposition, quoted by Jean Paulhan in his preface to *The Story of O* – now became the reality of O's life. The truth about the cloister of love was revealed: it was no more than a common brothel, a place where women were sold to businessmen; and Sir Stephen was nothing but a pimp and occasional murderer.

In the end even a sublime love ends up as a commercial arrangement, as if it were no more than a pre-arranged orgy. The Marquis de Sade turns his hand to scribbling romantic novellas: O, who had lived for the ecstasy of enslavement, became a submissive woman in only the most commonplace sense of the term – a tart.

It seemed improbable that she could avoid an apparently inevitable decline. The death that she had been promised seemed ineluctable. And after all, death would have been easy for her: she no longer loved. Now she was giving her body acquiescently, but without desire. Nothing distinguished her from the other girls at Roissy: even the chain that had hung between her thighs, that most intimate badge of her unique servitude, had been removed.

O, once incomparable, was henceforth interchangeable with any of the high-class harlots that fill the pages of the gutter press and are, it seems, the essential lubricant of the machinery of Government and of international commerce.

That her downfall was well-publicised caused O to feel no bitterness: all the scandals, the legal actions, had made her into a living legend, and she herself chose to annihilate the myth she had become.

And so we might have expected that this infamous woman, having become a piece of public property, would at least keep the peace from now on. It would be a logical inference; once revealed in their true colours, whores are supposed to respect the law of silence.

But O has returned. Here she is again: transformed, renewed, fulfilled. We might have thought she would have died of despair, or spiralled into a pit of torment — the ultimate sublimation of her passion, perhaps. But instead she is back — and in triumph.

Now O comes to the acts of love no longer as a slave, but as a mistress — a word which men tend to use without paying too much attention to its meaning. O, who used to donate her body to the whim of any stranger, who allowed herself to be scourged and abused, has become a controller of male pleasures. She is not, like Anne-Marie, the madam of a brothel, recruiting young girls and ensuring their docility. Nor is it enough for her to be on equal terms with the men whose paths she crosses. No: she must be superior to them.

Many things have changed since *The Story of O*. There was a time when women used to yearn to be Justine: this revelation is now recognised as a truism in the endless columns of feature articles that fill the newspapers and magazines of the western world. The female sex, after a century of repression under bourgeois values, is re-emergent. Woman is the subject of television broadcasts, of political debates, and of sociological diagnoses.

Carnality is the topic of the day. Perhaps that explains the hint of pathos that currently surrounds matters of the flesh. We must restore carnality to its rightful place — the darkness, the night.

Do amorous women still search for a master; do lusty men

desire a mistress? It seems unlikely: these are dangerous customs in an age when tenderness prevails over passion, sexuality overwhelms eroticism, and the peep-show seems infinitely preferable to the possible contagion of physical contact. The popular songs have got it right: love is a risky business; it can kill you.

In these pragmatic times we mistrust everything: even love scares us. We have chosen as our predominant values comradeship, and mutual understanding – in fact everything that is lukewarm.

The New Story of O reflects these changes in morality. Sexuality, and the excesses of sexuality, remain at the centre of the tale; but these practices and experiences are no longer enjoyed only as pretexts for punishment. The new woman that O has become has endowed them with new potential: the mastery of sexuality procures the mastery of the world, passion is an asceticism that opens the windows of self-knowledge. O competes with men in an arena in which they imagine a woman can never be their rival: O competes in the arena of Power.

The men that swarm around O live only for power. They went into business not out of a lust for lucre but because wealth is the measure of power. Everything else – politics, women, luxury – are mere accessories. Sir Stephen, driven by his obscure desires, hatching his plots in the shadows, is almost impotent; he employs lackeys to supplement his failing lusts. O, on the other hand, remains unassailable; she gives herself, but only as if by proxy. She denies herself the pleasure that she lavishes on others with such deliberate indifference.

The degradation, the floggings and the humiliations she had endured at Roissy had brought O to a supreme detachment, an impassivity worthy of the great mystics. Sex, love and the whip are beneath her now; instead she concentrates on the essential battle against men. She has no particular desire to watch the sufferings of her victims; but, deploying a brand of feminism more robust than that of the most militant activists, she intends to prove to men, and above all to the most powerful of men, that she can vanquish them – and that the secret of her strength is her intimate knowledge of their hidden predilections.

Every man, perhaps, dreams of an archetypal whore: O plays that part to perfection. She embodies this abstraction, and takes control of those who imagine they can exploit her vices. She forfeits the immediate thrill of sexual enjoyment in order to experience an even more delectable stimulant: absolute domination.

O, having explored to the limits of her own psyche, has an advantage over all those who judge themselves only by comparison with others. She is indifferent to money; and perhaps even power is not her ultimate objective. The explanation for her activities is to be found, without a doubt, in her relationship with Jane, the young American. It comes as no surprise that she imposes on the girl all the ritual stages of her own initiation. It had been the same with Jacqueline, and Natalie – and, incidentally, can this be the same Natalie that we find here, disguised as a servant and more submissive than ever? But O experienced strong feelings of identification with her old girlfriends; now all that has gone.

No – what matters now is the transmission of knowledge and power to women. O asserts the ultimate authority in a surprise ending that should come as no surprise. The frailty and fragility of men is all too obvious: all too often their sexuality transports them to places they claim they would never visit. And at that point there is no choice left to them but to seek happiness in slavery.

1

O was wearing, as usual, a tailored suit of grey silk. The hem of the pleated skirt swung against her stockinged shins. The scooped neckline of the jacket revealed a white linen blouse. Her only jewellery was a plain band of steel round the third finger of her left hand.

She disdained underwear. Her stockings were held up with garters. Beneath her clothes, her breasts, her buttocks and her sex were naked. This had been her custom since the first time she had been delivered to Roissy by Rene R, her lover.

With a leather handbag over her shoulder O was standing in wait near the revolving door of one of the tall glass structures that cluster at the outskirts of Paris: the structures in which businessmen fuel their expansionary dreams. The towers dominate the city as their inhabitants hope to dominate the world.

It was the end of lunchtime, and the offices were filling up again. On their way back to work men turned to stare at O. That slim figure; those pale green eyes; those lips touched with just a hint of wine-dark lipstick; she was provocative, that was clear at a glance, and all the more so because she seemed completely indifferent. O didn't go out of her way to please; she didn't behave like the girls who flirt with you in the street, who seduce you with a silent look. O simply made herself available to everyone, as she had learnt to do in the rooms of Roissy; it was a submissiveness that could be taken for insolence.

Although she had previously seen him only in a secretly-taken photograph, she recognised the man she was waiting for among a group that was hurrying towards the lifts. He

1

had black and slightly curly hair, and concealed his youthful looks behind tortoiseshell glasses. His light summer suit, like everyone else's, was of beige flannel; like everyone else he had one of the financial newspapers tucked under his arm.

O fell into step behind him. As he entered one of the lifts, O slipped in with him and pressed the button to close the doors. They were alone together. O waited. The man began to feel uneasy. Unnecessarily, he adjusted the knot of his tie. O's face was averted, her eyes downcast, as if she couldn't look at him.

'Which floor are you going to?' he asked, in a somewhat strangled voice.

'To the top,' O answered.

The man started the lift and leant against one of its mirrored surfaces. O stayed where she was standing, at the other side of the cabin, straight and motionless. The man became aware of her scent: bitter woods and marshland herbs, a sharp and wild perfume.

Luminous numbers indicating the passing floors flickered on the screen above the doors.

'Me too — I'm going to the top floor,' the man said. O made no reply. He wished she would give him just one look, just a glance to show that she knew he was there. 'The lift takes fifty-two seconds to reach the top. And I'm afraid that's not enough.' Then, as the young woman still said nothing, still looked away, he added: 'That's not enough time for me to seduce you.'

O looked up at the screen. 'You have forty seconds left,' she said.

'Forty seconds is useless. You must give me a bit longer than that. Have dinner with me tonight.'

'That won't be necessary,' O said. 'If you need more time, I'll give it to you.' She reached out and pressed the red button. The lift stopped. For the first time, O raised her pale green eyes to look into the man's. 'There you are,' she said.

The man looked down at her with a worried gaze. 'What do you want?' he said.

'Nothing that you don't want yourself,' O replied; and she placed one hand on his arm, leant towards him, and parted his lips with her mouth. His tongue searched for hers but she pulled away, smiled, and moved her hand down to rest against his trousers. His manhood hardened against her palm. The man tried to push her away, but she tightened her grip. Her delicate fingers unbuckled his snakeskin belt; she unbuttoned his trousers; and took his organ in her hand.

A bell started ringing: the alarm was programmed to go off whenever the lift was stopped between floors for more than twenty seconds. O parted her lips and brushed them along the man's jawline.

'I had better start the lift again,' she whispered. 'But I guarantee you'll be satisfied before we reach the top.'

The man made no reply. The lift moved, and the ringing ceased.

O enclosed the man's stiff member in her hand and, keeping her body a little apart from his, she alternately pressed with her fingers and then released his flesh. He could see into the opening of her blouse, where little beads of perspiration were forming in the valley between her breasts. Above the doors, the numbers continued their inexorable parade: thirty-two, thirty-four, thirty-six . . .The man was breathing heavily. He closed his eyes, and was unable to hold back a moan. O clenched one hand round the shaft and fondled the purple crown with the other. The man sighed and tilted his head backwards. Thirty-eight, forty . . . The top floor was approaching. He grabbed a rail: he was beginning to come, he could feel nothing but the young woman's insistent fingers; and then he felt only the gushing pleasure, the pulsing release of his orgasm. The lift stopped.

The doors opened. O left, her bag swinging from her shoulder, giving no indication that anything unusual had occurred.

The man was still trying to adjust his clothes when he was blinded by a flash of light. Of course — a photograph. He blundered out on to the landing to see who had trapped him; but nobody was there. All the identical corridors with their identical carpeting led to identical closed doors. The young woman, too, had disappeared.

The man shook his head; he was angry about being caught in a trap, and even more furious that he had failed to hold on to the mysterious beauty whose hand had given him such precisely timed pleasure.

As he recalled her manipulations he felt his groin begin to tingle again. He had known quite a few prostitutes; but not one of them had been capable of combining such sweet dexterity with such an air of detachment. Her fingers had played on his instrument with a virtuoso's skill; but it was her haughtiness as she performed that obsessed him.

The man sighed, adjusted his suit, and ran his fingers through his hair. Once again he looked like any other businessman as he made his way to the boardroom of the multinational conglomerate Capitol Industries.

Whether it was winter or summer, Gina wore the same outfit: a black leather mini-skirt; apple-green or cherry-red tights; and either a plain T-shirt or a light jumper which would cling to her breasts, the freckled slopes of which were always on display above her low-cut neckline. Gina was a secretary. She had realised at an early stage that neither her shorthand speed nor her command of languages would be the key to success in her career; but her trick of brushing her bosom against the backs of the necks of the executives of Capitol Industries while handing over a file had gained her the attention of all of the senior managers as well as countless invitations to dinner. She refused each invitation in the same way: with a bored smile, a word or two of vague regret, and a hint that one of these days, probably, she might make herself available; and each time the sighing supplicant would return to his office as happy as if his proposition had been accepted.

No-one knew anything about Gina's private life; but hypotheses, suppositions and fantasies flourished at Capitol Industries. Victor Bergil, the Marketing Director, liked to picture his boss's secretary living with her octagenarian mother in a gloomy, wainscoted apartment in the Avenue Mozart. Gina's mother, Bergil imagined, was a harridan who insisted that her daughter should return home each evening no later than eight o'clock; and Gina's only treat would be to accompany her mother on Saturday afternoons to an old-fashioned *patisserie* near the Trocadero where, amongst a circle of friends which diminished from year to year, the old lady recalled the ostentatious glories of the Third Republic.

And of course Bergil fantasised about Gina's solitary pleasures, the lonely activities that were all the girl had to enjoy once she had put her aged mother to bed and retired to her own bedroom. 'I can see her,' Bergil would say, 'as if I were watching her through the keyhole. She is coming into the room; she is bolting the door so she can't be disturbed. She stops in front of the mirror set in the mahogany wardrobe. She looks at her reflection for a long time; and then, inch by inch, she starts to remove her T-shirt. At first she exposes only her stomach, which is flat and smooth and freckled. She caresses the skin with her fingertips as if she were another woman, an inexpert lover exploring an unknown body. Then she stretches out the material and pulls it up to uncover the generous mounds of her bosom. She flattens her breasts with the palms of her hands, and I see her shiver slightly. Her fingers play with her nipples; she cups her breasts in her hands and takes each nipple between a finger and a thumb, squeezing and twisting the hardening tips. She releases her breasts and undoes her skirt, which slides down her thighs. She rolls down her tights, stopping to tousle the long curls that can clearly be seen through the fine silk of her knickers; and then she parts her thighs and, standing on one trembling leg at a time, she removes the red tights. She is now naked except for her white knickers; one hand caresses the material where it is taut across her buttocks, while the other is imprisoned under the silk, its painted fingernails playing with the trapped curls. Her lips are apart; her eyes are almost closed, but not quite: she is still watching herself in the mirror, as if she were watching someone else, as if the reflected hand so rhythmically moving belonged to her lover. She doesn't want to rush things; it's important not to come too soon. Her other hand is now inside her knickers, too, stroking her soft cheeks, circling closer and closer to the warm haven between her thighs. Her fingertips reach the place, they press, pinch,

6

pull, and almost penetrate. Quickly now, and almost furtively, she removes the knickers. She parts the lips of her sex, and pushes in one finger, and then two. As she twists her body in order to see herself from every angle, her hand diasappears into her flesh. She starts to moan, faster and faster, in time with the thrusting of her fingers; and finally she cries out from the depths of her soul. And with her eyes closed at last she collapses on the bed, with one hand still clutching the seat of her pleasure.'

This was what Victor Bergil used to say. His colleagues listened to him with tight throats and racing pulses. Only Moreau, the Director of Planning, remained sceptical. He had an alternative theory: he had convinced himself that Gina led a double life. By day she was a secretary; but at night he imagined her a fashionable prostitute, gliding along the Avenue Foch and round the Place de l'Etoile at the wheel of a white Mercedes. To Moreau, it was an obvious transformation: she didn't even need to change her clothing, except to remove her conspicuous tights and thus expose her rounded thighs in an invitation that nobody could resist.

And so that day, as Gina was distributing papers to the men sitting round the table in the air-conditioned boardroom, Gilles Moreau caught her wrist in his hand.

'Well then, Gina: how much?'

The girl decided to misunderstand the question; pushing her breasts in front of Moreau's face, she leant forward to point to a column of figures. 'The usual, *monsieur*, as you can see.'

Bergil, jealous of his colleague's audacity, quickly intervened: 'I have to ask myself whether these papers serve any purpose. They always contain much the same information.'

There was a general murmur of agreement. At Capitol Industries lengthy meetings which meandered round every topic were neither unusual nor taken seriously. Gina freed her arm from Moreau's grip and said, drily: 'I was told by Monsieur Botterweg to give the files to you. And I have to do as he tells me.'

Moreau hefted the bundle of documents, and sighed. Victor Bergil couldn't take his eyes off Gina's T-shirt. He could picture her breasts: full and firm and heavy, with a sprinkling of freckles, and tipped with thick brown nipples. He imagined enfolding those breasts in his hands; squeezing them, licking them, sucking them; sliding his throbbing member up and down between them. He groaned aloud, and was pulled back to reality by the sharp voice of Bernard Vielle, the young scion of an old family, who had joined the company through the old boy network.

'The only purpose of all this paperwork is to convince us that Botterweg earns his salary. If it weren't for the endless bumph we might start asking what it is he actually does with his time.'

Bergil jumped, almost as if he really had been caught fondling Gina's breasts. 'This time, I think you'll find things are rather different. One of these files is sealed, and marked *Top Secret*.'

Gina graced him with a mischievous smile. Bergil would no doubt have relapsed into one of his dreams about her had he not been interrupted by Gilles Moreau's contemptuous laugh.

'Daniel Botterweg likes nothing better than cloaking his actions in mystery,' he said. 'But I'll tell you something else, and unfortunately it's not "top secret": Pembroke is coming to France. And he's coming to buy us up. If we don't defend our position, he'll gobble up Capitol Industries – and spit us out.'

'You worry too much,' Bergil replied. 'Pembroke Senior was the big man, the real Pembroke; and he died five years ago. Against him we wouldn't have stood a snowflake's chance in hell. But we're dealing with his son; that gives us at least some hope.'

'From what I've heard, the son is at least as formidable as his father,' Moreau grumbled; and then the door opened, and everyone fell silent.

The man who strolled in had had time to recover his dignity. His face had resumed the expression of a decision-maker, and revealed no hint of his preoccupations or of his encounter with O.

Gina scurried forward to hold the door for him, but he didn't reward her with his customary appreciative glance. He threw his papers on to the conference table.

Gina pouted. 'Everyone is present, sir,' she said.

'So I see. You can leave now,' said Henri Carel.

Henri Carel was the Chairman and Managing Director of Capitol Industries. He had inherited an initial shareholding, and little else, from his father. Carel Senior had started his career as an army officer, posted to Indo-China and then to Morocco; and he had been in North Africa, and about to retire from military life, when he met Jeanne Duval. He was representing the army at a conference of missionaries, who regaled the assembly with reports on the progress of civilisation and the Christian faith among the savages. Delegates were reminded of the ceaseless travail of the peace-loving holy fathers, who risked their lives so that naked blacks would worship box-wood crucifixes instead of ebony idols. The conference was held at a church school for girls. The mothers had made biscuits which they served to the delegates; the native maids employed by the school took quiet satisfaction from watching the French women at this menial task. The group of army officers made it clear that in any other circumstances the honour of these part-time waitresses would be in no little danger. Lingering appraisals which turned into vacant stares towards the horizon spoke volumes about lively military skirmishes with yellow girls and black girls, expert whores and bashful innocents.

Jeanne Duval was one of the schoolgirls. She met Captain Carel at the fête held on the playing-field during the conference. She was wearing an unbleached cotton blouse with her initials embroidered in red above her left breast. She had overheard the dashing Captain as he narrated his military exploits. Like many officers, Carel had some talent as an actor, and Jeanne was enthralled by his adventures. Carel could hardly fail to notice her: she had the fresh face, the short straight hair, the shy but ready smile of a schoolgirl; but her figure, and her heavy breasts, were a woman's, and her steady, clear gaze seemed to promise to soothe his troubled spirit. As he reached the end of his narrative, he was speaking only to her: the rebel attack had been swiftly beaten back by the timely arrival of the Foreign Legion. The ladies applauded; the gentlemen expressed muttered reservations about the authenticity of the events described, as they had read nothing about them in *Le Temps* or *L'Action Française*. The captain swept away, taking Jeanne and leaving a faint scent of the sirocco.

He walked alongside her, whispering compliments designed to amuse young girls. He took her hand and brought it to his lips. And after a little while he held her by the wrist and drew her, in silence, into an empty cloakroom. He pushed her against the hanging coats, which promptly fell off their pegs. Jeanne started to giggle, and Carel pressed his mouth against hers to keep her quiet. Until that moment Jeanne had enjoyed mere rehearsals for such kisses: as an adolescent she had kissed schoolgirl friends, pressing her lips against theirs and persuading herself that she was in love. But she had never before been so besieged by lips and tongue, never so invaded and overwhelmed. After only ten minutes of such intimacies, she was sure that the captain was the only man in her life.

Jeanne Duval was the sole heir of her family's fortune; and her new husband soon started squandering it on various political schemes. After he had lost the third million an arrangement was made: he would be purchased a sinecure as Governor of Madagascar, and in return he would consent to a divorce. Jeanne was now thirty and had a son of eight. Carel promised himself a life of pleasure with nubile Malagachy women; but absinthe, malaria and untreated syphilis soon combined to make the young Henri an orphan. As he grew up he retained a soulful look and a serious demeanour which were to stand him in good stead in his later years as a businessman. He became a timid man, seldom convinced of his own abilities; and, as he had so little confidence in his own judgement, he never gave his word without making mental reservations — which made his promises worthless. He, at least, felt no obligation to stand by decisions that were conditional upon so many uncertainties. Practising these methods in the commercial world, Henri soon recovered the millions that his father had lost. And now Capitol Industries was one of the most flourishing European multinationals, with a bewilderingly varied portfolio of interests.

As usual, Henri Carel was followed into the boardroom by Daniel Botterweg, a little man of indeterminate age with darting eyes and a permanent slight smile on his lips. Botterweg was Henri's Special Adviser; his Mephistopheles, according to some. Capitol's competitors had tried to headhunt him on several occasions, but he remained inexplicably loyal to his young boss.

Henri Carel took his place in the large leather chair at the head of the table. He cast a worried glance over the members of the Board.

'Well, I heard you all laughing just now,' he said. 'At least that shows some spirit. I must confess that I'm not in the mood for laughter.'

'Is the situation really that desperate?' Moreau asked, while Bergil obsessively manipulated his pile of papers.

'Desperate?' Carel repeated. 'I should say it's terminal. James Pembroke has made up his mind to acquire this company. His visit to Europe is for that specific purpose. He is offering our shareholders ridiculous amounts of money: ten times as much as they're worth, fifteen times if necessary. I have to admit that if I were in their place I wouldn't hesitate for long. Just long enough to drive the bidding up, perhaps — and then I'd sell every Capitol share I could get my hands on.'

Botterweg, who was seated on the chairman's right, gave a discreet cough. Carel turned to him.

'You don't agree with my analysis, Daniel?'

'Oh yes, I do. But a battle is never lost until it has been fought.'

Carel uttered a bitter laugh. 'Oh, well said, Daniel! A brave speech. You know, you sound just like my father.'

The Special Adviser shook his head and looked hurt. In a thin voice, he said: 'I merely want to point out that I think I have a strategy to counter Pembroke's manoeuvres.'

Everyone in the room stared at him. Although they knew Botterweg as an unrivalled master of strategy, they could not imagine how he hoped to defeat the forces ranged against them.

'This must be our one last chance,' Carel sighed. 'Let's hear what you have to say, Daniel.'

Botterweg tried to stifle his smile. His eyes remained fixed on the Mont Blanc fountain pen with which he was drawing circles on a sheet of paper. 'Before I explain,' he said, 'I want to ask you to be as open-minded as possible. The weapon that I am about to suggest that we use is not normally found in the armoury of a respectable business. I fear that it might even seem so unorthodox to some of you — '

'Enough of this preamble!' Carel interrupted brutally. 'Get to the point, Daniel.'

Botterweg resumed: 'You all know, of course, what happened to Bloomingfeld and Pullerman, a few years ago in the United States?'

'It means nothing to me,' said Bergil.

'They were a couple of very big noises. On Wall Street it rained when they frowned, and when they smiled the sun came out. A crowd of small investors had absolute faith in them, and followed every step they took. Just like Pembroke's, their reputation was such that they had only to publicise the launch of a bid for a company for it to fall into their clutches. However: it happened that between one day and the next they were obliged to withdraw from their commercial ventures, take early retirement, and from then on live for the rest of their lives – presumably in no great hardship – on their accumulated savings.'

Vielle, who was still young and impressionable, asked in a strangled voice: 'What on earth happened to them?'

'A scandal, my young friend! These respectable businessmen were rather too interested in young people – of both sexes. There were revelations in the papers – including photographs – and the threat of court proceedings for the corruption of minors. They were ruined.'

Carel polished his glasses and then spoke. 'Daniel, you surprise me. What possible connection can there be between this old sex-scandal and Pembroke's public bid for Capitol?'

As even the Chairman had expressed incomprehension, the others felt encouraged to give vent to their agitated indignation. Moreau went so far as to remark, in an arrogant tone: 'I believe this is a waste of our time.'

'If you don't want to waste time,' Botterweg said, 'I suggest you stop your endless interruptions. Pembroke, as we all know, is even more puritanical than most American businessmen. He finances campaigns against abortion and

13

homosexuality. His publishing companies produce mass-circulation newspapers and magazines that never miss an opportunity to fulminate against moral laxity. He claims that he and his wife Sally, and their children Jane and Larry, are the model American family: fit, healthy, and God-fearing. Just imagine what would happen if we could tarnish that image. Imagine Pembroke caught in the act at an orgy! The press would love it.'

'I'm not happy with this plan,' Carel said.

'If you can think up a better alternative . . .' Botterweg replied.

'You win, Daniel; you're right. But how can you make someone like James Pembroke succumb to temptation? He's a block of stone, cold, hard and unshakeable.'

'He's the real thing,' Bergil added. 'He really believes in moral regeneration and all that born-again nonsense.'

'Some journalists have already tried to push girls into his lap,' Moreau said. 'Just for long enough to take a photo. But he's careful, and none of the dirt sticks.'

'I am well aware of all that, gentlemen,' Botterweg replied. 'But I intend to use an infallible weapon; a weapon against which no-one, man or woman, has any defence.'

'Well, what is this weapon?' Carel demanded.

'Just a woman,' Botterweg said.

The news was greeted with a burst of laughter. There could be no doubt: Botterweg had gone mad. Moreau and Bergil were already glaring at each other, sizing up the competition for the little man's position. But Daniel Botterweg was not easily discouraged. He fixed Carel with an intense look and said, in a firm but gentle voice: 'She's waiting in my office.'

Carel, with a sudden intimation of the truth, had difficulty swallowing. He tried not to blush as he said: 'Very well — we'd better take a look at your secret weapon.'

Botterweg pressed a button on the internal telephone and said: 'Gina, would you show the lady in, please.'

Everyone remained silent, impressed by Botterweg's handling of the scene. Carel tried to convince himself that Daniel would never have played such a mean trick on him; but he knew, as he waited for her to make her entrance, that she must be the same woman. It had to be her: the woman in the lift. And he had to admit that Botterweg was a genius. Because it was true: no-one in the world could resist the sexual magnetism of that supremely beautiful creature.

And if any further proof had been necessary, it would have been enough to observe the other members of the Board as O stepped through the door. They sat as if glued to their chairs, their eyes wide and their mouths dropping open. Gina seemed to be fascinated by O, and followed in her footsteps as if she couldn't bear to be separated from her.

Carel was aware that both O and Botterweg were looking at him. Later, he promised himself, I'll find out what there is between those two. But now, he had to restore his authority without delay.

'Well, Daniel — don't you think you ought to introduce your friend?'

Then he stood, took O's hand, and lifted it to his lips. The spell was broken, and all the Directors remembered to stand up to welcome their lovely visitor. Carel escorted her to the table, asked her to take a seat, and looked up to address his colleagues.

'And now, please excuse me. I have to leave the meeting. Daniel, please take the chair and carry on without me.'

As she sat, O lifted the back of her skirt, as she had been taught to at Roissy, so that her thighs and buttocks rested directly on the leather of the seat. She saw that Henri Carel had noticed; her green eyes held his gaze until he had to look away. As he left the room, he said: 'When you've finished, Daniel, please drop into my office. Gina!'

His secretary followed him from the room. As the door closed, he heard O's husky voice.

'Please, gentlemen, do be seated.'

Henri was in a state of nervous excitement. As soon as he was inside his office, he turned to Gina.

'Come closer!' he gasped.

She took a step towards him, and he plunged his hand inside her T-shirt and seized one of her firm round breasts. The secretary tried to pull away, but he snapped: 'Don't move!'

The young woman murmured, without much conviction: 'Oh, Monsieur Carel, please don't . . . '

He drew her body against his and took her lower lip between his teeth. She moaned, and he neither knew nor cared whether it was a moan of pleasure or of pain. With one swift movement he tore open the garment that covered her bosom, and when Gina tried to cross her arms he forced her elbows apart and rained kisses on the soft furrow between her breasts. He rubbed his rough cheeks against her nipples; he buried his face in the yielding mounds of flesh. His lips roamed down to her belly and then up again to her throat, which was scented with vanilla.

Gina had closed her eyes, and had rested her hand on Henri's head. She let her body rest against his. She felt her nipples stiffening under the insistent pressure of his tongue, and she slid a hand under her tights, across the small of her back, into her knickers, between the warm cushions of her arse, into the damp hollow below -and began to rub herself; while Henri went into ecstacies as he lost himself in her firm, rounded, tender breasts.

Gina's thumbnail was tickling the puckered skin of her anus; her index finger had reached forward to the meeting-point of the lips of her sex. She felt the pleasure growing within her until she felt she would burst; and then she came,

16

and couldn't restrain a yell, which caused Henri to jump. He pushed the young woman away, but she failed to understand that he was finished. She reached for his trousers, found his member, fondled it through the thin flannel, and was vaguely surprised to find it so limp. Carel tore himself free but Gina, assuming that his excitement was of a sexual nature, merely laughed, and grabbed his suit again, and started to unbutton his trousers.

'Stop it!' Carel roared; but Gina had already dropped to her knees to take him into her red-lipsticked mouth. This was too much for Carel and, although he had never struck a woman before, he slapped Gina with all his strength. She fell backwards, on to the carpet, and put her hand to her face. Five white fingermarks showed clearly on her cheek. Round-eyed, she stared up at him.

'Monsieur Carel!'

'I – I really am most terribly sorry,' he stammered; and as he went to help her to her feet, the door opened. Botterweg stood in the doorway. With one glance, the little man had seen everything: his boss red-faced and out of breath; the boss's secretary, naked from the waist up, lying on the floor. He extended a helping hand to Gina.

'You must have slipped, my dear. I'm always telling Henri that this carpeting is treacherous.' He turned to Carel. 'You asked to see me?'

They were alone now in Carel's office. The vast plate glass window overlooked the Seine and the massive outline of the Trocadero. The river was reddened by the setting sun. Carel dropped into an armchair, and Botterweg handed him one of the dossiers he had circulated at the board meeting. He extracted a photograph of O sitting in a straight-backed Louis Quinze chair. She was wearing a silk suit that clung to her body; the garters at the tops of her thighs were just detectable. She was looking scornfully into the camera as if mocking any onlookers; one fingernail caressed her lower lip.

Carel studied the photograph. At last he said: 'Daniel, it's in your own interests that you succeed.'

Botterweg shrugged. 'O is irresistible.'

'Quite so,' Carel said. 'And as for the snapshot you took in the lift, I would have expected you to let me have the negative — without my having to ask.'

Botterweg put on an injured expression. 'The entire photograph is already in the drawer of your desk,' he said.

3

The avenue, bordered by box hedges, crossed a formal garden. Behind a pool in which swam ageless carp the chateau arose like a mountain. It was a huge edifice of white stone and slate roofs; its round towers and gothic windows dominated the landscape. Each successive occupant seemed to have been determined to leave his mark by adding a wing here, a terrace there, or a battlement elsewhere. The overall effect of this haphazard architecture was a surprising harmony, and the chateau had an insidious charm that no visitor could resist.

That day, at dusk, three black limousines entered the long avenue. They were driven by chauffeurs in black livery. James Pembroke occupied the first car; he was sitting in the back, and his attention strayed from his telephone conversations only when he had to consult his lap-top computer or dictate a memo into his recording machine. James Pembroke often said that every second had a value – in dollars – and he hated to lose money.

In the second car was his wife, Sally, an opulent blonde whose every finger was weighted down with gold and gems. By contrast the two Pembroke children, Jane and Larry, riding in the third vehicle, looked like a couple of average students. Larry was chewing gum conscientiously while peering out at the park, which was already being engulfed in darkness. Jane, more thoughtfully, was wondering what a seventeen-year-old would find to do in the midst of all this medieval antiquity. She intercepted her brother's gaze; he had been staring at her bare bronzed thighs. She tugged at the hem of her short skirt to no effect. Larry was a weird kind of guy, she reflected; he was twenty years old, wealthy, had the looks of an American football pro — but he seemed to have no interest in girls, except for his own sister, and Jane thought that didn't count. Jane was still a virgin; but she was ready to bet that she'd already kissed more boys than her brother had kissed girls.

As Jane Pembroke mused about her brother, the three limousines reached the end of the avenue and stopped in front of a pink marble staircase. Two servants were waiting at the top of the steps. The man was fair-haired, with the face of a Greek god: a straight nose, a strong chin, and smooth cheeks. He wore a black, waisted jacket and tight-fitting black trousers, and it was clear that he had a perfect body. The female domestic was equally agreeable: laughing and mischievous, she was the living image of a 1920's pastel drawing of a little *Parisienne*, effervescent and giggling in a wasp-waist corset and garters. She had flaming red curls and was wearing a black outfit that revealed her dimpled, stockinged knees as well as the upper slopes of her prominent alabaster breasts. The corset and garters could be imagined without difficulty.

The male servant descended the staircase and opened the door of the first limousine. James Pembroke stepped out and stopped to look up at the chateau. His wife and children joined him. Larry couldn't keep silent.

'Wow! Would you look at that? That's just awful.'

'This is pure Hollywood,' Sally Pembroke added. 'This is just like a film set.'

James Pembroke smiled, an expression that looked out of place on his austere face with its cropped hair and stiff moustache. 'The difference is that here,' he said, 'it's all real. Let's take a look inside.'

They followed the liveried servant. At the top of the stairway the maid greeted them with a small curtsey.

'This is Natalie,' said the servant. 'My name is Pierre.

20

Madame has instructed us to place ourselves at your service – as we are at hers.'

They passed through the carved stone arch and entered the chateau. In the vast panelled rooms with ornate plasterwork ceilings, canvases by Dubuffet and Braque rubbed shoulders with Boudin watercolours. There were Renaissance tapestries, and furniture by Bugatti. There were Greek statues, Ming porcelain, Etruscan pottery, and a fresco by Balthus. Pembroke, who hoarded paintings in the cellar of his fake medieval castle near Houston, shouted his satisfaction.

'Good old Europe! There's still plenty of treasure here to buy. But that's enough time lost. Pierre, where's the phone? You got a fax here? I'm not here to do the tourist bit, I've got business to attend to.'

'Honey,' his wife said, 'I'd like to take a look around this typical French condo.'

'There'll be plenty of time for that, Sally – after all, we're going to be living here.'

'Natalie will take you on a tour of the property, *madame*.' Pierre said.

'OK, but what about my phone?' Pembroke complained.

'A telephone point has been installed in each room, sir. If you wish you can use the library, or our Mistress's office.'

'Hell, no. I like to use my own room.'

'Very well, monsieur. We thought that the Prince's Suite would be most suitable for you; and we propose, for Madame, the Unicorn Room.'

Pembroke looked quizzically from one servant to the other. A look of suspicion crossed his face, and a belligerent tone entered his voice.

'Two rooms? Separate rooms? What the hell's that for?'

'It is customary, *monsieur*.'

'Since the day we were wed my wife and I have shared

21

the same bedroom. Just like every good American couple that's been legally joined in the sight of God and their fellow men. And I don't see why I should start changing my ways.'

Pierre and Natalie exchanged a look, as if they had met with an unexpected difficulty. The maid turned to Pembroke and spoke hesistantly.

'If you please, *monsieur*, in olden times the husband and the wife had a bedroom each. There was enough room, you see.'

'That's not the problem.' Pembroke was obdurate. 'I'm telling you: we'll share the same room.'

Sally gently placed a hand on her husband's arm.

'Oh, James, come on. We're not in America now. Let's go native. Let's do things the European way. It'll be so romantic — and for once in my life I won't have to put up with your damned cigars and your all-night phone calls to every place around the world.'

Pembroke frowned, paused for thought, and then burst out laughing.

'OK, Sally. Have it your way. We'll sure have some fun finding each other, anyway.' He placed a kiss on his wife's forehead and said to Pierre: 'Right. Let's move.'

'If Monsieur would be good enough to follow me,' the servant said; and Sally and the two young people watched as Pierre led Pembroke up a colonnaded staircase. Larry grabbed his sister's arm.

'What about that guided tour? Where do we start?'

The girl pulled herself away. 'Why don't you go with Mom. I'm exhausted. That journey's killed me. All I want is a bath and a bed.'

'You're making a mistake, little sister. Night time's the right time to look over an old pile like this. It's only the daylight that keeps the ghosties away.'

Sally shivered. 'That's quite enough, Larry.'

'You're scaring us,' said Jane.

'But ghosts aren't dangerous, are they, miss?' Larry asked Natalie.

'That depends,' the maid said, 'on whether or not you mean them any harm. But don't worry: there are no ghosts here.'

'That may be so,' said Sally, 'but, Larry, your sister's right: it's too late to look the place over tonight. We'll all be fit for it tomorrow. Natalie, would you take us to our rooms.'

'Of course. We will start with Mademoiselle's room — the Eglantine Room.'

'What a wonderful name!' Jane said. 'Did you choose that room for me?'

'Oh, no. It was Madame — I mean, our Mistress. It is always Madame who makes the decisions.'

'Whoever it was, she's done a great job,' Sally said, stifling a yawn.

Left alone, Larry made his way towards the marble statue which had attracted his attention as soon as he had seen it. It was an ephebus, a young Greek of about Larry's age, completely naked, his hand raised as if in greeting or invitation.

The statue was so realistic that, if it hadn't been for the pallor of the stone, it seemed inevitable that the young man would move. Larry, almost against his will, spread out his fingers and rested them on the youth's thigh, where the muscles stood out tense and lean.

The contact with the marble made him tremble. A strange emotion gripped him; his breath caught in his throat. He remembered this feeling; he had experienced it two years previously, at Princeton. He had just played in a particularly fierce baseball game. And whatever you could find to criticise in Larry Pembroke — he was certainly neither gifted nor over-zealous as a student — he always put his heart and

23

soul into sport. This wholesome enthusiasm, together with the cheques his father paid to the old students' fund, ensured his popularity. In the unanimous opinion of his teachers Larry Pembroke was a worthwhile person, even if he did think that Thackeray was a brand of gin and that Cleopatra had been invented by Elizabeth Taylor.

So, on that sunny May afternoon heavy with the perfumes of spring, Larry had played hard and had helped his team to victory. Dripping with sweat he had rushed into the shower; and then the cubicle door had opened and Loostel was standing in the doorway, naked, his thick black penis surrounded by a bush of even darker curls. Loostel had the body of a supreme athlete; he was supposedly under consideration for the next Olympics. His ebony skin glistened and his smile was an array of gleaming teeth.

'Hey, you still in here, Pembroke?' he had said.

Suddenly, Larry had felt awkward. He had mumbled something like: 'I'm almost through.'

Loostel had shrugged his broad shoulders. 'No problem. Don't rush on my account. There's no shortage of shower cubicles.'

He had made no move to close the door. He had just stood there. And Larry, unable to keep his eyes away from the hard, muscular, black body, had felt his own penis begin to harden. His voice emerged as a strangled hiccup.

'It's OK. You can have this one.'

And without stopping to turn off the water he had rushed out of the cubicle. As he had passed the big black man his pale, half-erect member had brushed along the dark, muscular thigh. Loostel had merely smiled, mockingly, serenely sure of his strength and beauty; and then he had shut himself in the shower cubicle and, with the easy conscience of the true sportsman, he had begun to holler his own version of *Blue Suede Shoes* while the water poured over him.

Outside in the dazzling sunlight Larry had suddenly realised that he was naked, and had hastily covered himself with a towel before sitting on the grass. His pulse had been racing; there had been a pounding in his temples. Never before had he experienced a sensation like that — not even when he had grappled with Phoebe Zimmerman on the back seat of the Cadillac. His thoughts had filled with unwelcome questions that he had immediately repressed.

'It's the heat, that's all. Just the heat, and the excitement of winning the game. No need to look further than that.'

Now, touching the cool marble body of the ephebus, he rediscovered that sensation: a knot in his intestines and a weight against his chest. He placed his hand on the front of his jeans; his crotch was enlarged, hard and tight. It's nothing, he told himself; nothing but the effects of the long journey and this crazy castle.

He continued his solitary tour. He stopped in front of a picture which, he decided, must have come from the Middle Ages — although in fact it was a copy of a Watteau, depicting barely-clothed young women playing at being shepherdesses. Elsewhere he found a tapestry representing courtly love; and a fin de siecle table with mahogany feet carved in the shape of women's bodies.

Larry felt himself falling under the mansion's spell. He seemed to hear music emanating from the ceiling; but the sound was so faint that he couldn't tell whether it was real or a product of his imagination. In the same way, he detected the scents of incense and myrrh without being able to discover their source.

For a while he felt the urge to retrace his steps; as he ventured into the depths of the chateau he began to think that anything could happen, that quite unbelievable events were possible in this place. He felt a sudden presentiment of danger: he and his family were in danger. But the feeling passed.

25

'I'm being ridiculous. I tell a few ghost stories to frighten Jane, and here I am getting scared by a few rooms full of antiques.'

Larry found himself in a large room with a red-tiled floor. The whole of the far wall was a glass-fronted bookcase full of leather-bound volumes. A log fire was flaming in the raised fireplace; there were beige leather armchairs and a small round ebony table. But the strangest item, positioned in the centre of the room, was a statue of pink-veined marble that represented Diana the Huntress. At first sight the pose was completely classical; but there was something unusual, something frankly carnal, about this figure of the goddess. It was as if the woman who had posed for the statue was present in the room; as if the naked flesh of the real woman, rather than her stone image, were being offered to visitors.

Like all young men, Larry had seen pornographic videos, and girlie magazines, and peep shows — he kept these things secret from his father, of course, because James Pembroke would have raised the roof if he had found out. In any case Larry had remained largely unmoved by the forbidden sights he had seen. But here, looking at the statue, he realised that he had never seen anything quite so lewd and shameless.

Fascinated, he walked round the statue, marvelling at the detail of the goddess's legs, and of her hips, and of her buttocks. Suddenly he heard the heels of a woman's slippers clicking on the tiles, and the room was filled with a bright, white light. Larry blinked and recoiled as if caught doing something wrong. He heard a voice — Natalie, the maid.

'Were you looking for something?'

The maid attached a mischievous grin to her question. Her wide lips, outlined with rouge, were an invitation to kiss and bite. Larry took another step backward, as if afraid he might succumb to the temptation.

'No, no. Nothing at all. I was just taking a walk.' And

26

then, almost in spite of himself, he added: 'I just love that statue.'

Natalie moved to stand beside him. She sighed, and Larry couldn't avoid peering into the neckline of her dress, where her breasts were rising and falling.

'We all love her dearly,' said the maid.

'Is that so?'

'She is so beautiful.'

Larry timidly extended a hand towards the marble woman. He touched her knee, and started to stroke it without realising what he was doing.

'It's almost as if she's alive.'

'But she is alive, *monsieur*!'

'What are you talking about? This piece of rock has to be two thousand years old.'

'Not at all. On the contrary, the statue is very recent.' And quietly, as if telling a secret, Natalie added: 'It's the Mistress – it's O'

'It's who?'

'My Mistress – Madame O. The house belongs to her.'

Larry withdrew his hand as if the stone had suddenly burst into flame.

'And I was thinking it was a museum piece,' he said.

Natalie took hold of his wrist. 'Close your eyes; let yourself go . . . ' she instructed.

Larry knew that he should resist, but he allowed the maid to pull his hand towards the statue. She placed his palm on a thigh, and then guided his hand across the lowest part of both buttocks, and then between them, and on, up the spine, veering towards the ribs, across the belly and around each breast.

'There,' she whispered, as his fingers brushed a marble nipple, 'that's the way to understand this statue. Not with your eyes, but with your hands, by feeling the grain. You see here – at the neck, at the base of the neck – you feel

27

how the texture changes? The stone is rougher, and much older.'

'Right, it is,' said Larry, his eyes still shut.

'The head is from the fourth century BC. A friend of Madame O, a sculptor, had the idea of restoring the statue with the Mistress's body as his model. He was quite right. She is so perfectly beautiful.'

Natalie couldn't help giving Larry's hand a sudden squeeze. Surprised, Larry broke away.

'You, uh — I guess you like her a lot.'

'She is adorable,' Natalie said.

Larry now took the maid's hand, pulled it towards the exquisitely rounded curves of the statue's rump, and with the girl's languid fingers traced a slow line round and beneath the cold convexity.

'Maybe we could — '

'No!' Natalie said in untypical earnest, looking straight into Larry's eyes. 'The answer is no, Monsieur.'

'Hey, I didn't even say — '

'It was quite clear to me, Monsieur.' Then she laughed. 'I wish you good-night, Monsieur.'

Larry placed a hand on the black lace at her shoulder. 'So that's a final "no"?'

'Well . . . you'll find that here "no" means "perhaps"; and "perhaps" is as good as "yes"; and "yes" might as well be "all the time" . . . '

Larry released the young woman; she turned and walked quickly away. He recovered his self-possession. 'Well, that's all I need to know,' he called out to her. 'Now I know the code, you can bet I'll use it. Nightie-night, Natalie!'

She had already disappeared. The tapping of her heels was fading into silence. For a few moments he stood, deep in thought, before the statue; then he moved very close to it and, having made sure that he was alone in the room, he pressed his lips against one of the Huntress's cool, soothing

28

arse-cheeks. He stayed there a long time, resting his fevered lips on the icy recesses of the statue's rear end; he failed to see Pierre, who was watching from the shadows with a thin smile on his handsome face.

4

Sally had changed into her most expensive night-wear: an almost-transparent gown of sheer silk. Had she, like her son, been affected by the strange atmosphere of the chateau? Was it the sensuality of the place? Or the intangible presence of the Mistress of the house? Without planning to, Sally had spent a long time luxuriating in the bathroom. She was sure that her husband would come to her when at last he finished his wheeling and dealing.

In one of the dressing-table drawers she had found a complete array of cosmetics. She found some oily rouge, too dark to use on her face; but she scooped a little into the palm of her hand, without thinking about what she was doing, and rubbed it with a circular movement of her fingers. And although she had never before done anything of the sort, it occurred to her that she could use it to emphasise the aureoles round her nipples, which she could not help noticing were pressing their dark points against the soft material of her night-gown. The rouge seemed to have very little affect at first, as she used both hands to push aside the silk and then with rouge-covered fingertips manipulated the large russet ovals round her swelling nipples; but the colour deepened with time. She thought she had used too much, and caused her nipples to shrink to flinty points as she applied alcohol in an attempt to dilute the rouge; but it had little effect, and she decided to start all over again, massaging more of the unguent into the summits of her two soft hills of suntanned flesh. Her nipples were as crimson as blooming peonies.

Considerably aroused by this novel approach to using

make-up, Sally had no difficulty in persuading herself that she should also highlight the hidden lips of her sex. But the rouge failed to show up on the moist folds of flesh, and after some time, and reluctantly, Sally abandoned the idea. Instead she sprayed herself with perfume from a vapouriser she discovered in another drawer. She watched the mist liquefy against her skin, trickling between her breasts and clinging in droplets to her golden triangle of curls.

'And now I'm all ready,' she said to herself.

She sat, watching the door, on the edge of the bed. This was a large, square piece of furniture, very low and with a covering of furs. Behind it, across the entire wall, was the tapestry which gave the Unicorn Room its name. Sally found her eyes once again drawn to the remarkable scene depicted in glowing colours of shimmering thread. A crowd of people, all of them naked or clad only in thin veils, were touching and embracing each other as they watched the spectacle in the foreground: a woman, naked and in chains, was apparently about to be ravished by a unicorn which displayed both male and female characteristics. Sally stared at the picture for a long time. Above all she was fascinated by the stripes across the woman's buttocks; and she was struck by the deliberate vulgarity of the scene — as if the artist had poured all of his skill into displaying the exact position of the animal and its helpless victim. Sally could not help estimating the size of the beast's erect phallus and, with a shiver of delight, she imagined it ploughing the furrow between her arse-cheeks and thrusting into her belly.

The soft skin of the woman's breasts and stomach was also marked. Sally had heard that sometimes women were beaten, and that some of them derived pleasure from the pain. She would never allow herself to be treated in such a manner; but somehow, in that bedroom, she felt an indefinable yearning, and then she suddenly realised that she, the respectable and sensible Sally Pembroke, wanted, for perhaps only a little while, to be the heroine of an pornographic story.

The door was violently flung open. With a determined stride, James Pembroke advanced on his wife. Sally raised her hand.

'Couldn't you knock before you walk right in? You gave me a fright.'

'Knock? I should knock to get into my own wife's room?'

All of Sally's fantasies dissolved like mist. She wasn't the heroine of an erotic romance; she was the legitimate wife of the rich and powerful James Pembroke. She sighed.

'But this isn't home, sweetheart. While we're here we have a chance to behave differently. We should make something of having separate rooms. I know: why don't you go out again, and knock? Just to please me? Three secret little knocks, like this, so that I'm the only one who can hear them. That would be so romantic!'

James gave him wife an exasperated look.

'Sally, you know I don't have time to waste on that stuff. I haven't come to France for some sentimental journey. I'm here on business. My money is my power.'

'But I'm not interested in power.'

'Maybe not, but you're happy enough to live on it. And you live damned well, let me remind you.'

'It's not enough, James'

'Well, I sure as hell don't understand what you mean. You've got everything you could possibly want. You've got comfort, luxury, influence. You've even got a husband who still treats his wife to everything she asks for, after all these years we've been together. There aren't so many wives who can claim all that. What more could you want?'

'Manners, James; style, refinement. I guess you'd call it "packaging".'

James shrugged, undid his belt and produced his rampant

32

member. He grabbed his wife's shoulder, pulled her to her feet, and pressed his body against hers.

'Come on, honey,' he grunted, 'that's enough talk.'

Sally forced him away. 'You think you can just bust into my room and come on like I'm some thousand-dollar tart?'

James gave a scornful chuckle. 'A thousand dollars? Darling, you have absolutely no idea about prices,' he said, at the same time trying to pull up Sally's night-dress. Sally struggled against him, and there was a quiet but unmistakable sound of tearing: the thin material had been unable to withstand the strong hands that clutched at it. Sally surrendered.

'OK, OK, you're tougher than me. You can have what you're here for. But that's all you get.'

She slipped out of the torn silk. She was well-built and buxom, but with a shapely figure and smooth, suntanned skin that was golden rather than bronze. Her narrow waist flared into a rounded belly, wide hips, and a large ripe peach of an arse; her bosom was big and heavy. James noticed that her nipples appeared to have been painted red, and for a moment he wondered whether he'd missed something; but Sally gave him no time to think about it. She lay on the bed, burying her face in the furs, spread apart her knees, and lifted her hindquarters for her husband's inspection. She knew that this was his favourite way to have her; and she knew that he always felt guilty about it. She raised her eyes and thought she detected a sort of complicity in the face of the woman in the unicorn tapestry.

James studied his wife's arched back and outthrust arse. Lust coursed through him. Without looking round, Sally murmured: 'What about it, Pembroke?'

He knelt behind her, angry without knowing the cause, and mumbled: 'You're right. We won't waste time.'

With one sudden thrust he forced himself into her narrow passage. Sally cried out in pain, and provoked a frenzy in

33

James. He wrapped his arms around her, slid one hand across her stomach and began to rummage in her fleece of curls. At the same time he lunged brutally in and out of her; and he expected her to put up with his brutality — it was, after all, only the most obvious of the ways in which he demonstrated his power over her.

James thrust like a pile-driver between his wife's buttocks. Her passage widened to accommodate him as she raised her body slightly and his hand moved to cover the wet gulf between her legs. In spite of herself Sally was overwhelmed by a wave of pleasure. She had been invaded from the front and from the rear, by a hand which thrilled the interior of her belly and by a sword of flesh which transfixed her.

But apart from this hand and this rigid organ with which she was only too familiar, there was something else that provided extra excitement: Sally was sure that she was being observed by someone — someone who was involved in her mounting gratification. The woman in the tapestry was watching with an intense and understanding gaze as Sally, in the throes of physical extremity, clamped her mouth to her arm in order to stifle her cries.

Sally was making love to the eyes of the woman in the tapestry, and not to the panting, groaning man behind her who, increasing still further the tempo and violence of his thrusts, let out a raucous yell at the same moment as Sally felt a burning wave flooding the lower part of her back.

Then Sally hid her face among the furs, so as to avoid the searching eyes in the tapestry, and let herself come with a long drawn-out wail.

Her husband collapsed across her back and bit her, leaving tooth-marks on her shoulder.

'That was worth more than a thousand dollars,' he gasped.

James had gone back to his room to call Tokyo or Washington. Sally turned over, sat up in the bed, and then leant against the pillows as she gently trailed a hand along the length of her slit and between her buttocks.

She still felt that she was being watched, and for a few moments she caressed herself for the benefit of the woman in the tapestry. She turned to make sure that the woman was watching her, but the face now seemed lifeless, and the eyes were no different from those of the minor characters in the tapestry.

Disappointed, Sally let her hand fall on to the sheet. She pulled the furs over her body and, before falling asleep, she realised that without intending to she had deceived James that evening — and that she had rather enjoyed the experience.

On the other side of the wall a woman was carefully applying rouge to her lips. She smiled, as if she had been responsible for organising the night-pleasures of the American visitors. O liked her guests to feel at ease in her home.

5

Dressed in beige trousers and an open-necked white shirt adorned with a blue silk cravat, Pembroke, the following morning, felt more like a country gentleman than a business tycoon. For a while he allowed himself to think that this was indeed the good life: the towering, leafy trees in the park, the ancient forest beyond, and the ornamental lake glittering in the sunlight. And also the delicious odours of breakfast: coffee, croissants, home-made conserves, all served on a service of silver dishes and antique porcelain. He looked at Sally, and then at Jane, and was filled with pride. As she ate her breakfast with the unstinting appetite of the young, his daughter's small white teeth flashed in the light; she was confident of herself and of her good looks. In a lemon-yellow tennis skirt that revealed most of her rounded bronzed thighs, she was the very picture of youthful health and beauty; and James considered that, if she hadn't been his daughter, he could easily fall in love with her. She had just the right sort of mischievous looks that could drive a middle-aged man to the most outrageous stupidities. Sally's eyes were ringed with pale shadows that raised all kinds of questions about her nocturnal activities; but her lightly-clad body, glowing and sensual, perfectly suited the luxuriant style of the ancient domain.

However: this was not the time to start dreaming. As far as James Pembroke was concerned, there was never a time to start dreaming. In every corner of the world, at every hour of the day and night, there were terms to be negotiated, contracts to be drawn up, competitors to be outwitted. This fellow Carel . . . He wouldn't hold out for more than three

36

days. If he had the sense to quit without a struggle, Pembroke would be generous. He would offer him a well-paid sinecure in one of his subsidiaries. Dozens of his former competitors had become his employees in this way, and had been able to maintain their executive life-styles — but at Pembroke's pleasure. That power was one of the many satisfactions that money bought.

James reached for the telephone, stabbed the buttons, and gestured to Sally to pour more coffee for him. As soon as the connection was made — on this occasion it happened to be with Dallas — he thundered: 'I got your telex. It's out of the question. It was up to you to do something about this . . . What? And what the hell do you think I pay you for?'

Jane leant forward and allowed a piece of croissant to slide underneath the table. There was a loud growling and an enormous dog, as dark as pitch and with coal-black eyes, dashed from beneath the table. It was James's Dobermann; his bodyguard and his only confidant.

The dog leapt towards the girl as she jumped from her seat. She waved another fragment of croissant and laughed: 'Catch, Bruno!'

The animal bounded round her, yelping and slobbering and revealing an impressive set of jaws. As she twisted and turned, teasing the dog, Jane's skirt flew up and displayed glimpses of her slim hips and the curves of her bottom. She shouted and laughed at Bruno. James covered the mouthpiece of the telephone with his hand and said: 'Let's have some quiet, you two! Jane, stop teasing the dog!'

The girl threw what was left of the croissant to the Dobermann, who ran to pick it up. In the ensuing silence James finished his conversation and put down the telephone.

Jane, out of breath, sat down beside him; the Dobermann approached her again, his body trembling with excitement.

'Bruno didn't come along to play games,' James said, 'he's here to protect us. He's no lap-dog, he's an attack dog. Watch out or he'll bite you.'

Jane spread butter on a slice of bread and held it out to the Dobermann, who snatched it from her hand. 'I don't understand you, father,' she said. 'You're always saying that a dog has only one master. Well, you're Bruno's master but you never find the time to play with him.'

James shrugged impatiently. When the dog once again threw himself at his daughter, he ordered: 'Here, Bruno! Heel!' And the Dobermann immediately came to lie under the table at James's feet.

The dog was still for only a few seconds. He lifted his head, his ears cocked towards the forest, and he let out a ferocious roar.

'Now what?' James said. 'Sit down, Bruno!'

The multi-millionaire stood up and saw a horse galloping from the woods. He could make out the silhouette of the rider, who was sitting very straight in the saddle and guiding the horse towards the chateau. On reaching the park, the horse slowed to a trot.

'I thought we were guaranteed some privacy here!' he complained, and grabbed the telephone. He dialled a number and yelled into the mouthpiece.

'Pierre! Get down here to the terrace. At once! I want to know what's going on.'

'So you haven't invited anyone?' asked Sally, sarcastically.

'This is no guest. This is an intruder. Get inside, both of you. I'll deal with this.'

Accustomed to doing as they were told, Sally and Jane stood up and went towards the house. Meanwhile, the horse was drawing near. James saw that the rider was a woman; an exceptionally beautiful woman, he realised, with a calm face but a keen and piercing gaze. She was dressed in a full skirt of brown wool, a tight-waisted jacket, and black gauntlets that reached her elbows.

O brought the horse to a halt in front of Pembroke, who, belatedly, made a gesture to restrain Bruno; but the dog was already calm. Standing squarely on all four paws, the Dobermann lifted its head towards the horsewoman as if waiting for her instructions.

James advanced on the stranger and in a haughty tone demanded: 'How did you get in here? We don't take kindly to being disturbed − do we, Bruno?'

O dismounted, revealing snakeskin boots with gilt spurs at their heels. James had to admit he admired her style, but her attitude angered him. O gazed at him with her pale eyes.

'Do you have any sugar?' she said.

'On the table.'

O pushed aside the American with the tip of her riding crop and plunged her hand into the silver sugar-bowl. She took three cubes of sugar and turned back to her horse, throwing one cube to Bruno, who caught it in mid-air, before feeding the other two to the horse.

As if she sensed Pembroke's increasing fury, and was enjoying it, she made no haste to explain herself. But at last, without turning round, she said: 'I have not come to borrow your sugar, Monsieur Pembroke − although I believe I have read that that is one of the excuses that Americans use to make the acquaintance of new neighbours . . . '

She turned and graced him with an icy smile. James was astonished: no-one dared to treat James Pembroke in this manner. This woman was either stupid or monumentally insensitive . . . or extraordinarily clever. She was saying: 'The fact is that you are my guest. This domain belongs to me. I am O.' Her smile faded. 'An appointment was arranged for this morning. I fear you have overlooked it.'

James suddenly realised that he was in the wrong. He covered his embarassment with a forced laugh. 'That's right!

But don't expect any apologies. I've never been known to say I'm sorry.'

'That makes two of us, Monsieur Pembroke.'

'OK, let's forget it. And please accept my invitation to join us for breakfast.'

'With pleasure.'

James pulled up a chair for her but she chose another, facing him. She sat as she always did since her days at Roissy, lifting her skirt so that she was exposed from her waist to her boots; she shivered as her buttocks rested on the cold metal of the seat. James noticed that on the third finger of her left hand she wore an unusual ring – a plain steel band decorated with three golden spirals – but he made no mention of it. At that moment Pierre stepped on to the terrace and, on seeing O, stopped in his tracks. Jane and Sally appeared behind him and they stood , too, trying to get a good look at the mysterious visitor.

James poured a cup of coffee and passed it to O, who acknowledged it with a flutter of her eyelashes. 'I don't believe,' she said, 'that there is any need to discuss the house. I have left Pierre and Natalie for you, and I am sure that with them you will find everything will go well.'

'No doubt about it,' James replied. He had to admit that this woman had enthralled him. An irresistible influence, a magical sensuality, an almost hypnotic seductiveness surrounded her. He knew instinctively that he had come face to face with someone just as strong and ruthless as he was, and he recognised that she would achieve her ends by employing methods that were different from, and perhaps more subtle than, his own. Without being able to define his fears exactly, he sensed the existence of forces that were even more potent than money and politics. O knew of such forces; she was mistress of them. And the extent of her control over the world and its inhabitants surpassed James Pembroke's.

The telephone rang. Automatically, the tycoon picked it

up. 'Yep? What? Oh . . . Yeah, yeah, she's here.' Surprised, he passed the receiver to the young woman. 'Seems to be for you.'

'Thank you,' O replied. During her conversation, she kept her clear green gaze on the American. Her voice was nonchalant but firm.

'Yes, certainly I want you to buy . . . You can go up to two million . . . Yes, but do it with a little discretion, I don't want to draw attention to what we're doing . . . OK. Call me back.'

She hung up. James burst out laughing. 'What currency are you dealing in?' he asked, in a tone that he intended to be contemptuous. 'Italian lira?'

O touched the rim of the coffee cup with her lips. In this slight gesture, somewhere between a bite and a kiss, there was an unavoidable challenge. Her voice remained cool. 'In dollars, Monsieur Pembroke. Genuine greenbacks. It's one of the rules of the game: serious business is conducted in serious money.'

'This is mighty fancy talk from a woman who's just bust in on me like some primitive warrior queen. You're not telling me that you're in business as well?'

'Commerce does not interest me, Pembroke. Power is not bankable. I love power, Pembroke. I cannot get enough of it.'

James realised that he was hanging on to this woman's every word. He placed a hand over his eyes as if to counter a momentary spell of dizziness or to dispel a disturbing thought. He beckoned to his wife and daughter, and said to O: 'I'm not at all sorry we've had this little meeting. This is all very interesting.'

'Indeed, Monsieur Pembroke,' said O, seriously, 'it is very promising.'

Sally and Jane were accompanied by Pierre, who maintained the respectful and distant demeanour expected

41

of a butler. As they approached, the Dobermann scented Jane, rose to his feet, rubbed against her legs and then started to snuffle under her yellow skirt. Embarassed to be seen playing with the dog so intimately, Jane made a bad-tempered gesture and tried to push him away.

'That's enough, Bruno! Down! Lie down!'

The dog's head was completely underneath the short strip of material, lifting it to reveal skimpy cotton knickers that failed to cover the girl's buttocks and through which her blonde bush of hair could clearly be seen. Jane tried to seize the dog by its collar but he growled and tried to bite her. Almost in tears, she pleaded with the animal; but Bruno continued to nuzzle the tops of her thighs and Jane, tormented more by being the centre of attention than by the activities of the dog, did not dare to move. She appealed to her father for help.

'Dad, please! Do something! Call him off!'

James lifted his hand and was about to order the animal to heel when he caught O looking from Jane to Bruno and from Bruno to himself. It was a knowing and amused look, revealing a remarkable insight into the situation. James felt his throat tighten as he admitted to himself that, for a few seconds, it was he, James Pembroke, through the vicarious means of his pet dog, who had sniffed underneath his daughter's skirt. In a rage, he clicked his fingers; but O had anticipated him. Almost inaudibly she had said: 'Heel, Bruno!'

The dog hesitated; then, whining, came to lie down at O's feet. Jane straightened her skirt and, feeling that she should say something, mumbled: 'I don't know what's got into that stupid mutt.'

'I told you not to play with him,' her father complained.

Sally looked at him in surprise: surely that shrill, strangled voice wasn't her husband's? She suddenly decided to take a closer look at the strange horsewoman; and she was obliged to conclude that she had never before seen such a delightfully attractive creature. And the creature knew it: O wore her riding habit with an elegance that was almost insolent.

Now O rose from her chair and extended a hand to Sally. 'Monsieur Pembroke has omitted to introduce us,' she said, 'so I shall introduce myself. I am O; and this is my house.' She turned to Jane. 'You and I have never met, but I know many things about you – as I do about all of your family.' And, taking Jane's hand between hers and pressing it warmly for some time, she added: 'I am very happy to know you.'

James could hardly believe it. This young and now completely affable woman, who was playing the role of the mistress of the manor and creating a sort of instant coalition among the womenfolk, seemed to have nothing in common with the one who, only a few minutes earlier, had been dictating telephonic commands and claiming to love nothing but naked power.

He decided that from now on he would be on his guard against O, and not only because her very existence offended all his principles. A man like James Pembroke couldn't afford the luxury of doubting himself or his ideals; not even for the duration of a brief romantic interlude.

Meanwhile, Sally was unable to restrain her enthusiasm: 'Well I do declare,' she gushed, 'you really are the most wonderful intruder we could have wished for!'

'What do you say?' demanded O.

Sally could only wave her arms, as if dismissing her words as worthless foolery: 'Oh, nothing; nothing at all. We sure are happy to know you, too. But tell me: how did we get to hear about each other?'

'And,' James added, 'why did you lend us this place? It sure can't be for the rental!'

'It is all very straightforward,' O explained. 'An old

43

friend, Sir Stephen, asked me whether I could make you welcome for a few weeks. I've never done that for anyone before, so naturally I made some enquiries before making my decision.'

'I hope the answers were favourable,' James said with a strained laugh.

'Monsieur Pembroke, the whole world knows about you!'

Sally took O by the arm. 'It's a real delight to know you,' she said. 'If it's OK with James, would you like to stay for lunch?'

'I was going to ask you myself,' the millionaire grumbled.

'I'll tell the servants,' said Sally, turning towards Pierre.

'It is not necessary,' O said. 'Everything is already arranged.'

James bit his lip. This woman scored points in every round she played, and that worried him. For the moment it was just a game of trivialities; but although he had no evidence for his fears, he suspected that these skirmishes presaged a deadlier battle.

However, he could only admire the charming way that O included Jane in the conversation. 'What a pretty outfit! Did you intend to play tennis this morning?'

'Oh . . . yes, but that lazybones of a brother is still in bed.'

'You and I could play after lunch, if you'd like to.'

Jane felt her heart beat faster. This is silly, she thought, she's only inviting me to play tennis. But O was so charming, so magnetic, that nothing to do with her could seem ordinary. Jane hesitated, her gaze wandering to her new friend's perfectly-formed and perfectly-coutured body. O merely waited for the girl's reply with the patient calm that had been instilled in her at Roissy.

'OK,' Jane said eventually, in a small voice.

As if he understood the significance of this agreement, Bruno fidgeted under the table. James gave him a furious kick.

O seemed not to have noticed the disturbance, and she asked, perhaps almost too politely: 'It won't bother you, I hope, if Pierre goes to fetch my tennis things?'

'Not in the least,' James replied. 'And anyway I've got things to do before lunch. So please excuse me; you know as well as I do that you can win or lose everything in just a few minutes.'

Violently, he pushed back his chair. O looked up at his face; or perhaps at the vein that was throbbing in the centre of his forehead.

6

Jane and O played tennis for an hour in the brilliant sunshine. O contented herself with returning the ball from the base-line with unfailing skill. Jane ran back and forth along the base-line and up and down the court, giving an occasional shout of frustration when she missed a lob or was wrong-footed by a particularly fast and accurate shot.

She knew that O was watching her as she flung herself about the court. Her cheeks were red, her hair was flying all over the place, and her shirt was soaked with perspiration. She was out of breath and, when she stopped running for a moment, her legs felt cool with dampness. She was completely exhausted when O finally said: 'Shall we take a rest?'

'I'd love to,' Jane managed to say between gasps of breath.

They sat together under the shade of an oak, on a spectators' bench beside the court. Jane had recovered her breath, but neither of them spoke. Jane felt O's eyes on her. Was she imagining O's expression of tenderness and desire? She wondered whether O looked at all women in this way; perhaps, at school, O had yearned for the girls in their brief tennis skirts and thin shirts. Jane's small, upthrust breasts, set high and wide apart on her heaving chest, were visible through the damp material. Her firm, tanned thighs and her disordered blonde hair gleamed in the dappled sunlight. Did O want to tear aside the shirt, place love-bites on those high breasts, push them together with the palms of her hands, toy with the rose-pink nipples?

And in fact, O had always had a taste for women. Not

in order to flout convention, although it did amuse her to embarass her girlfriends by kissing them full on the mouth in the street or in a restaurant. And not for the thrill of the chase itself, however delightful and romantic it could be. No: she found that love between women conferred a complete freedom that she rarely experienced with men; a freedom that she enjoyed to its utmost. There were few women that she did not find attractive; and many were, she thought, at least as beautiful as she. There was nothing that gave her more pleasure than to hold a woman in her arms, to enfold her naked body and gratify her desire, while O herself did not even remove her clothes. She had discovered some time ago that pleasure does not necessarily require reciprocity, and she left it to the authors of erotic fiction to invent those co-ordinated bouts of organised passion in which all of the participants achieve simultaneous ecstasy. The laws of lust, she had learnt, are altogether more uncertain, more unbelievable, and certainly more compelling than that. The lessons that O had learnt from Rene, and then from Sir Stephen, could not be put into words; but they had revealed to her the power of being a woman. And she intended to communicate her knowledge to those that she deemed worthy of being initiated.

Jane brought her hand to her upper lip to remove the droplets of sweat that had gathered there. O intercepted the girl's arm, leant towards her, looked into her eyes, and brushed her lips across the girl's mouth. Jane didn't move. She felt a stirring inside her, an emotion that was much stronger than the excitement she felt when a boy pulled her into a corner during a smoochy track with the lights turned off at the end of a disco. It was more intense even than the sensations she enjoyed when she caressed herself at night, falling asleep with one hand still curled over her blonde sex.

'You smell good,' O whispered.

47

'I smell of sweat,' Jane protested, 'I'd say I smelled yucky.'

'Not at all. You know nothing about it yet. Every person's skin has its own odour. I think you smell good.'

O buried her face in the girl's straw-coloured tresses, breathing in the scent of her. She kissed the nape of her neck, moved her face along the shoulder, and placed her lips on the bare skin at the top of the girl's arm, where a patch of wetness stained the shirt. Jane wanted to push O away, but the woman looked up and ordered: 'Don't move.'

Jane knew she should just stand up and walk away. After all, she didn't have to let herself be bossed about by this strange woman who seemed to be able to control everyone in the place as if she owned them. But a more insidious force held her back − more than mere affection or fascination − it was an inexplicable desire to do everything she could to please O.

'Your smell tells me all about you,' O went on, 'I can read your body like an open book.' And at the same time she placed her hand on Jane's thigh, and caressed its light covering of blonde down. 'You are fully grown,' O said, 'but you are also still a little girl. And still a virgin, aren't you?'

She stroked Jane's knee and the insides of her thighs. The girl wanted to close her legs but O's hand obliged her to keep her thighs apart. She gave a nervous laugh. 'You know, you're really something. You talk business with my father like you're his attorney, you bewitch my mother with a bunch of Old World clichés, and with me . . . With me you're doing this. I mean, I didn't expect − at lunchtime you were doing your dashing horsewoman bit . . . '

'Do I frighten you?' O said.

'No, you don't scare me,' Jane replied; and then, after a pause, she said: 'No. That's not it. I think I like being frightened by you.'

She looked at O, her eyes wide and her lips slightly parted. O covered the girl's mouth with hers. Jane didn't pull back but she didn't respond to the kiss. O extended her tongue, delicately probed the girl's mouth and touched her tongue. Jane could not help herself: she reciprocated O's pressure, pushing her tongue and lips against O's. Jane's taste of salt and spearmint mingled with O's bitter-sweet flavour; their breaths combined. After a while, it was Jane who was the first to break away from the kiss; but she did nothing to stop O sliding a hand under her skirt.

'You're right,' she said, 'I am a virgin. And I'm happy that way.'

O's only response was to press her hand against the tender, hidden flesh. Jane caught her breath as O placed her fingers against her knickers, which were moist with both perspiration and desire.

'You can't tell me you knew I was a virgin just from my smell,' Jane said. 'That's crazy.'

O moved her slow fingers back and forth across the thin cotton, from the start of the pubic hair to the hidden furrow below, increasing the pressure from time to time. Jane was breathing loudly; her cheeks were flushed. She tried to close her legs around O's hand, but O gave each thigh a light slap to keep them apart. Jane began to be overcome by an irresistible desire for O to pull aside the knickers and enter the secret gash between her fleshy lips. To counteract her yearnings she began to talk again, very quickly.

'So you've made enquiries about us. Well, you said so yourself. There's nothing clever about that: our family is well-known and highly respected. There are no black sheep in our family, no skeletons in our closets. When we get married, everything is decent and honourable, and that's what I'm going to do, and I'm proud of it. As for your stories about smells – '

'They are not stories,' O said, and pushed her second

finger against the front of Jane's knickers, inserting the material between the girl's secret lips; and then she moved her finger gently but insistently. Jane closed her eyes, but only for a moment. She felt O's green gaze on her, and found the courage to look into her face. O gave her an approving smile.

'You are still a little girl, and you don't know everything. Here in France our wine tasters can determine the origin and the year of a vintage by smell alone. They have no need to drink. They are guided by their noses, not their palates. Most people have lost the use of this sense; they think they have to use deodorants. It is all nonsense.'

'I always use a deodorant,' Jane said. 'I don't want to smell nasty.'

'You will stop immediately, from today. And you will smell wonderful: the smell of your body, your secretions, your desires.'

With her other hand O unbuttoned Jane's shirt. She looked at the pert, swollen breasts, and then applied her lips to each nipple in turn, following the outine of the aureoles with the tip of her tongue. Meanwhile her fingers moved faster underneath the girl's skirt. Jane started to tremble, and moaned very quietly, and was suddenly inundated by a wave of pleasure that swept over her all too quickly. O stilled her hand but left it resting between the girl's thighs.

Jane put her head against her friend's shoulder. Although the urgency of her passion had been asssuaged, she still felt inflamed with desire. Only the kisses, the stroking, the presence of this woman could satisfy her. In a small voice she said: 'You were talking about scent . . . '

O fondled the girl's breasts, pushing them together and teasing the small pink nipples. 'You have very pretty breasts,' she said, 'smooth and golden and completely unmarked, so far.'

'So far?'

'You will find out, as I did. I think you will enjoy it. You will enjoy it as shamelessly as I, in time.'

'I don't get it. What about scents,' Jane insisted. 'How does a virgin smell?'

'Your odour is already heavy and full of sensuality, surprisingly so in such a young woman. But in the background of these grown-up scents, there is a sort of acidity – the scent of an unripe fruit.' O withdrew her hand from beneath Jane's skirt and placed her fingers against the girl's upper lip. 'Here – smell yourself.'

Jane inhaled. She could smell O, but above all she scented the odours of her own body, intimate odours that reminded her of her recent pleasures. 'And do I smell good?'

'Of course. But you are not yet complete.'

Jane looked grave; almost unhappy. 'I know,' she murmured.

She started to rebutton her shirt, but O forbade it: 'No. I want to see your breasts.'

'But what if someone comes . . . '

O made no reply at first, but put her arm round the girl's shoulders. 'Keep your hands at your sides,' she said at last, 'and your legs apart, like that. You will become accustomed to it. You don't want to deny your body to me, do you? It doesn't matter if you feel ashamed at first. You will find out, as I did, what it is to be humiliated and happy at the same time. There have been others . . . but I will tell you all about it one day. For now, just keep still.'

Jane chewed on her lower lip. 'I – I didn't tell the truth just then, she said. 'I haven't kept my virginity because I wanted to stick to Daddy's principles. You know he uses his family just like he uses everybody else; we're pawns in his power games. For political reasons it's useful for us to have this image, the ideal American family, healthy and united, strong and pure. It doesn't bother me, but I'm beginning to dislike it.'

O stroked Jane's arm, and the girl was encouraged to open her heart. Jane had never before felt this close to anyone. It was a comfortable feeling, even though pangs of guilt worried her. She knew that all she had to do was to stand up and say 'Let's go back inside.' O wouldn't try to stop her. This freedom to act, or not act, entirely according to her own wishes was a new experience for the young American, and it worried her more than O's caresses.

'You can probably guess,' she went on, 'I've had plenty of opportunities — plenty of offers. But I always wanted something more; something better; something else. I can't put it into words.' She looked directly into O's eyes. 'But now that I've met you, perhaps I know. I wanted it to be like a tornado, so that I couldn't resist; so that I was swept away, turned over and over, drowned, lost. I wanted ecstasy — I wanted everything sucked in, eyes and mouth, body and soul. I wanted to be sure that afterwards, nothing would be the same. You've lived through that, O. You're not like all the others. Teach me.'

O removed her arm from the girl's shouders. 'Stand up,' she said firmly.

The girl obeyed, almost without thinking. O frowned. 'You are asking for a great deal, Jane. The tornado you desire does exist. But you have to recognise it as it approaches and you have to find the courage not to run away. It is less easy than you think to let yourself go, to allow yourself to be swept away. You have to serve a long apprenticeship. And you are right: I have lived through it, several years ago now. And I will tell you all about it one day; I will educate you.'

'Now!' Jane begged.

'I cannot believe that you are ready,' O said; but she appraised the girl standing beside her. Jane's long, slim legs were set apart, her breasts jutted defiantly. O seized one of them, and squeezed it. She took the nipple between her

52

thumb and forefinger, and gradually tightened her grip until she saw the girl's eyes close in pain; and then she pulled, stretching the breast into a perfect cone. As she released the nipple, her other hand swung in a wide arc and delivered a vicious slap to the lower part of the girl's left buttock. Jane neither moved nor cried out.

'Well. Perhaps you are ready, after all. When I was in your situation I had a lover who acted as my guide. I could do the same for you; but you must have absolute trust in me. If you don't want to go through with this, I won't mind. But if you accept my offer, you must stay with it to the very end, without question, and you must obey every command I give you.'

Jane knew that she was going to say yes. But it was still the most difficult thing in the world to say it. Her throat was dry. O, staring into the blue sky, waited as patiently as ever for the girl's answer.

'OK. I agree.'

'You consent to be my pupil?'

'I agree to do everything that you want me to. I trust you, O.'

'In that case, we'll start immediately. First, you must know that I shall come to you when you least expect me; and you must always be ready. That means that you must always be naked underneath your skirt. So get rid of those knickers. You will never wear them again.'

The girl hesitated. O's voice was harsh. 'Jane, this is not a game. You can pull out now if you want to. But if you don't, you must do as I say.'

Jane lifted her skirt and pulled down her cotton knickers. They dropped to her ankles and she bent over to pick them up. 'Stay like that,' O said. 'Don't move.'

O lifted the girl's skirt and folded it back across her waist. She inspected the buttocks, which were slim but well-rounded; she shaped her palms to the swelling flesh that overhung the tops of the thighs, and delivered a few gentle slaps, and her smile suggested her satisfaction at finding the curves firm and yet supple enough to move when beaten. She caressed the very soft skin at the topmost part of the inner thighs; she parted the buttocks with the fingers of one hand while the other explored the contours of the valley in between. She inserted a fingertip into the puckered orifice, and Jane gave a start of surprise. O kept the girl in this position until she was sure that Jane had become used to being put on display, examined, handled like an animal in a country market.

'Stand up,' O said at last, and Jane straightened. Her face was red and tears of shame glistened in her eyes, but she smiled at O, who said: 'Whenever you sit down, Jane, and wherever you may be, remember to lift your skirt like this. Your skin must be naked, and in direct contact with what you are sitting on. As you sit down you will be reminded that you are naked for me; that you are mine in perpetuity.'

O pointed to the bench on which they had been sitting. 'I'll show you,' she said; and raised her skirt and placed herself on the wooden board. She stood up again. 'Now you.'

Obediently, Jane lifted the hem of her short skirt and sat on the bench. She shivered on contact with the wood; but could not tell whether it was the coldness of the bench, or a thrill of fear, or some other sensation that had affected her. 'I feel exposed,' she whispered, 'as if everybody can see me and do whatever they want with me.'

'You are beginning to understand,' O said, leaning down and placing her mouth over the girl's. They exchanged a deep kiss which O abruptly terminated. As she turned to walk away, she said: 'Don't forget, Jane. I will come for you when you least expect me.'

7

Outfitted once again as a horsewoman, with her riding-crop under her arm, O burst into the room that James Pembroke had chosen as his office. He was tapping at the keyboard of a computer terminal and spared scarcely a glance for O. In a preoccupied voice he asked her: 'You had a good time with that daughter of mine?'

'We enjoyed ourselves,' O replied.

'She's a fine girl; and such an innocent little thing. Which proves that a wholesome upbringing makes for a wholesome personality, as I'm sure you'll agree.'

'She certainly plays very well,' O said with exaggerated gravity; and although James pretended not to notice the intonation of O's words, he was aware of their ambiguity. He resumed his manipulation of the computer keyboard, as if to indicate that he had sacrificed enough time to the requirements of etiquette.

O extended her hand between his face and the number-filled screen. 'Thank you for your hospitality, Monsieur Pembroke. Now I have to go: I too have work to do. And don't worry, I won't disturb your peace again. My house is yours for as long as you want it.'

James stood up, took O's hand and, after a moment of indecision, brought it to his lips. 'No, please, be our guest,' he said, 'come over whenever you like. Sally was just thrilled to see you. But if you want to see me, phone first to make sure I'm here.'

O turned to go, her spurs jingling at each step; but she stopped next to a chess table. 'These pieces have been re-arranged,' she said. 'Do you play chess, James?'

He pointed at the computer. 'Only with this. I don't have a human partner at my level.'

'Then you must have a game with me,' O said.

'Well I'll be darned! Riding, tennis, and now chess — seems to me there's no end to the games you play well.'

'The friend I spoke of this morning — Sir Stephen — taught me to play. Sometimes one game would last for days at a time. But then, we were playing for stakes that justified the extraordinary duration of our games.'

'And what were the stakes you were playing for?'

'Can't you guess, Monsieur Pembroke? Power — we always played for power.'

'Now you're talking! You're right — we must have a game.'

'Whenever you wish.'

'How about right now?'

O looked pointedly at the computer, the telephones, and the piles of papers. James made a dismissive gesture. 'Forget that. It isn't every day that I come across an opponent like you.'

He stood up and joined O at the chess table. Bruno, who had been lying at his feet, stretched, yawned, and followed him. As O moved to meet the dog, James clicked his fingers: Bruno stopped, pulled back his lips, and snarled. Without hesitation O placed her hand on the Dobermann's head. 'Bruno,' she murmured, 'your turn will come, too.'

James was placing the chess pieces in their positions on the table. 'What was that?'

'Nothing — it's just between your dog and me.'

James laughed. 'Well, that won't stop me finding out. Bruno has no secrets from me. And anyway — there aren't many folks I can't find out all about, you hear me? I can find out everything.' He picked up the black queen and the white queen and concealed each of them in one of his clenched fists, which he displayed side by side in front of O. 'Choose!'

O pointed to his left hand. James opened his fist. 'White. That means you start.'

O made a standard opening and started to develop a attack on one side of the board. James was finding it hard not to smile: he knew the corresponding defence and how to counter-attack. As he captured one of O's knights, he asked: 'You said you used to play chess with power as the jackpot. What exactly does that mean?'

'In a game of chess, James, there is no room for chance or bluff. Nothing is hidden, there is nothing that has to be guessed or estimated. Luck plays no part in it. Each player has complete responsibility for his own success or failure, for maintaining the challenge to his opponent.'

'I get it,' James said, 'and the loser can see defeat coming from a long way off, right? He reaches a point where it's inevitable, and there's nothing he can do about it. Every defensive move he makes only weakens his position. The winner imposes his will. The loser doesn't just lose, he has his face pushed into the dirt.'

O castled on her King's side. A predatory gleam flashed in the millionaire's eyes, but O seemed not to notice his expression, and said: 'The winner becomes the master. The loser is the slave precisely because he cannot escape his fate. Chess contains a truth, a clarity, that is missing from everyday life − except in the case of certain very unusual individuals.'

James hesitated; then came to a rapid decision and moved his queen forward. 'In real life,' he said, 'you don't have to show your hand. In fact the more you bluff the stronger your position. That's why the game of real life is better than the game of chess, young lady, and don't you forget it. Unless − unless, I guess, you could find two people who'd face each other and play with every card face-up on the table. Now that would be what I call a dangerous game.'

O took her king and slowly laid it on its side. 'Well, as far as I am concerned, I am not prepared to play here and now. There — you have won.'

'I knew I would, right from the start.'

'But then, so did I,' O replied. She stood up, and before her skirt dropped back into place she revealed an expanse of smooth white skin. 'Now you will have to allow me to have my revenge,' she said.

'Whenever you like. I'm always ready.'

As she left the room O nearly collided with Sally Pembroke, who stopped in surprise and stood in the doorway looking from her husband to O in confusion. O placed a furtive kiss on her cheek. 'Don't forget our date,' she said, her green eyes fixed on Sally's face.

Sally stepped back, as if suddenly frightened. 'Your eyes — ' she whispered; she had recognised that cold yet sensual gaze. These were the eyes that looked down at her from the tapestry in her bedroom; this was the look that had devoured her while James had sodomised her the previous night. This gaze had drawn her into sexual ecstasy; with these eyes she had betrayed her husband.

An expression of amusement crossed O's face, but her voice remained disarmingly innocent. 'My eyes? There's nothing very special about my eyes.'

Sally put a hand to her forehead. 'Oh gosh, I'm sorry. I just had the strangest feeling. A sort of *déjà vu* . . . '

'It's those goddamned novels,' James shouted. 'You've always got your nose buried in some book. I'm not surprised they put ideas into your head. I'm always telling you, Sally, you read too much. A decent woman has no call to spend her time reading.'

Sally gave a contrite smile. 'My husband's right. You're right, honey. It must be the journey. I feel a bit tired.' She made her unsteady way towards the kitchen, where she

58

hoped Natalie would make her a cup of tea. There's nothing like a cup of tea, she told herself, to set your ideas straight when you're starting to feel old in an ancient house haunted by strange phantoms.

O's emerald gaze followed her progress; and then O left the house, apparently unaware that Bruno was at her heels.

Even when on horseback O was careful to lift her skirt from beneath her, so that the skin of her thighs and buttocks was in direct contact with the leather of the saddle. She experienced riding as no horsewoman ever could without riding naked.

Bruno was trotting through the park, behind the horse. The dog didn't growl, and he was not in any way threatening; but he was looking up to watch every move that the young horsewoman made. He looked ready to jump up at her at the slightest provocation.

O turned in the saddle. 'Well, dog, you are determined to make sure that I leave, aren't you?'

The Dobermann halted and stood rigidly to attention. O reined in her horse and dismounted.

It was a sultry afternoon. There was hardly a breath of wind, and the only noise was the barely-audible buzzing of insects in the undergrowth. O sat at the foot of a tall beech and rested her head against the trunk. The dog, unmoving and confused, simply stared at her. 'Come here, Bruno,' she ordered quietly.

Bruno didn't move. 'Come here,' O repeated; and slowly, suspiciously, the dog took a step towards her. O made no other sound or sign; but carefully, so as not to frighten the animal, she spread apart her legs under her long brown skirt. Bruno looked at her with moist and gentle eyes.

'Come on, then, boy,' O said, with authority in her voice, and the dog obediently approached and stood in front of her. O spread her legs wider and bent her knees as if she

59

were preparing to accommodate the body of a man. She spoke softly to the animal, which pricked up its ears. 'Be gentle with me, dog,' she said; and the Dobermamm groaned. She placed a hand on his head and stroked him as if her were no bigger than a puppy, and by stroking him she lowered his mouth towards her opened legs. She whispered in his ear. 'Listen to the music of my voice, Bruno. You can't understand my words, but you can sense my meaning. Don't be afraid, Bruno. Come closer.'

O lifted her skirt from her thighs and folded it across her waist. Her sex, naked, open, and completely hairless, was exposed before the dog. Bruno growled once, and then buried his head between her legs. O positioned the dog's mouth, judging its movements by the feel of his breath against her skin. 'Lick, Bruno. Sniff. Jane wouldn't let you, would she? But I'll give you everything.'

The dog's rough tongue lapped the furrow between her legs. She raised herself from the ground and guided the animal's mouth to the crease between her buttocks; she used her fingers to separate the lips of her sex so that Bruno could lick the salty taste inside her; and at last she rested, smiling, against the trunk of the tree, and let the dog snuffle and tongue her at will. 'We'll be friends, Bruno,' she said, 'friends for always. And in a way that you can't be friends with a man – not even with your master, James Pembroke. You are mine. We are lovers, Bruno. You know, dog, that you have almost made me come? It's our secret, Bruno: you belong to me. I am your mistress now.'

The dog whined and lifted its great head to stare into O's eyes. O stroked his head, and then gave him a pat on the shoulder. He took a step backward, and O stood up. 'Sir Stephen once told me that I was a wanton, Bruno. An easy woman. Perhaps you think so too. But you are wrong. I am the most demanding of women.'

She took her horse by the bridle, patted its flank, and

remounted. Bruno looked up at her imploringly. 'But we have one thing in common,' she said to the dog, 'we are both oblivious to shame.'

She touched her spurs to the horse's sides and galloped into the forest.

8

The Japanese restaurant was in Neuilly, near the Bois de Boulogne. O had chosen it: she loved this district with its quiet streets of stone-built mansions, at the gates of many of which police guards stood to protect the wealthy and eminent inhabitants, and in which the same leafy avenues were the habitat of an exotic wildlife of ageing prostitutes in white sports cars and garish transvestites who yelled their conversations at the street corners. O revelled in the incongruity of the mixture: the *haute bourgeoisie*, with their marble porches illuminated by pale wall-lights and decorated with green foliage, rubbed shoulders with the sleaziest elements of the sex business.

She also knew that Henri Carel, making his way from his apartment near the Trocadero, would be unable to resist stopping his car for a moment in order to sample the services offered by the district's street-dwellers. Gripping the steering-wheel in his fists he submitted to a quick but rapid blow-job.

But it wasn't this experience that had put Carel into a bad-tempered humour. Nothing in the restaurant was to his liking: not the raw fish, not the background music, and not even the mysterious smile of the waitress in the blue kimono. Botterweg, as imperturbable as ever, was enjoying his yoshima, skilfully manipulating the slivers of octopus and squid with his chopsticks. For the tenth time Carel complained about the low seats and the awkward position he was obliged to adopt. 'I can't stand it any longer,' he said. 'My legs are seizing up. You can't sit like this unless you're born to it. It comes with the slanty eyes. What I need is a proper, well-upholstered chair.'

'I wasn't born in the Far East, you know,' O said, 'but I can manage this quite well. In fact I rather like it.'

'That's because not all of us can spare the time to visit sports centres and fitness clubs. And anyway running the business is enough to keep me in shape.'

'There are other ways to maintain the suppleness of the body.'

Carel stared at her, but O had resumed eating as if nothing unusual had been said. Botterweg refilled their glasses with Chablis. Carel shook his head and said to O: 'Everything about you is a mystery. Why should we put our faith in you? We've made a deal, but I don't even have the slightest idea of how far you've got with Pembroke.'

O savoured the bouquet of the wine and then touched the liquid with her lips. 'Perfect,' she said.

'Perhaps a little too chilled?' Botterweg suggested.

'The cold brings out certain elements of the flavour. I particularly like that touch of acidity that is almost hidden behind the bouquet.'

'It is still rather young,' Botterweg continued, 'but, unlike most people, I find that I thoroughly enjoy certain growths when they are still almost green.'

'Well, Daniel – we know your predilections,' O said with a smile.

'For goodness' sake stop it, both of you,' Carel shouted.

'So you don't agree?' O said. 'You prefer wines that have had time to mature in their cellars – and time, of course, to appear in the wine guides, so that there's no danger of committing a social solecism when making your choice. I must say that's exactly what I would expect of you.'

Carel choked on a mouthful of food. He was trying to capture a ball of rice between his chopsticks but it kept

63

escaping and rolling across the table. He picked it up with his fingers and stuffed it into his mouth. Still chewing, he said: 'We're not here to listen to lectures about viticulture!'

'Talking about the meal is integral to enjoying it,' O said. 'The same rule applies to other shared pleasures: we appreciate our experiences more, and in a heightened degree, if we talk about them as they are happening.'

Carel rapped on the table, and the waitress in the blue kimono appeared immediately. '*Monsieur*?'

'Oh – nothing, forget it,' said the businessman. 'Wait a minute, yes: bring me a fork. A civilised implement for normal human beings.'

He turned to find O looking at him. He thrust his face forward and tried to outstare her, but he could not prevail against her sparkling emerald gaze. He lowered his head and insisted: 'I've had enough of philosophy. I just want you to tell me how you are handling things.'

O placed her fingers on his wrist and, in spite of himself, Carel felt his insides tremble. 'This is not in accordance with our agreement,' she said. 'I was given to understand that you would ask no questions about my methods.'

Botterweg concurred. 'That is the case, Henri. I gave O an assurance to that effect.'

Carel gave him a venomous look. 'Sometimes, Daniel, I wonder whose side you're on.'

Botterweg shrugged. 'Yours, of course, Henri.'

Carel grunted doubtfully and then turned once again to interrogate O. 'No more prevarication, O. How are you doing with the American? He's made his bid. Capitol has three days at most to avoid the take-over.'

'Shall we say that I am making progress, Henri.'

'That's not good enough. I'm paying you well – very well – and I have a right to expect results.'

'Hasn't Daniel told you?' O said, her eyes wide. 'I'm not interested in the money. I just take it – that's all.'

'You're not interested in the money? And you expect us to trust you? This is madness. Daniel, it was a mistake to follow your advice.'

'And I maintain,' Botterweg said, 'that I've never had a better idea in my life. But how can I convince you?'

O produced an envelope from her handbag, opened it, and gave Carel a photograph and its negative. It was a shot of O and Carel in the lift: she standing a little apart from him, her fingers curled round his upright member. 'Perhaps this will convince you,' she said.

Carel took the photograph and examined it closely before showing it to Botterweg. 'I thought this was your piece of trickery, Daniel.'

O retrieved the photograph and returned it to her handbag. 'Only I have this photograph. Until this moment no-one else knew of its existence. That's why you have to trust me.'

'That's too easy,' Carel protested. 'One photograph is meaningless. What matter to me now are your motivations. Why are you doing this?'

O smiled, and made no reply. Instead she indicated to Botterweg that she would like her wine glass refilled. Carel was insistent: 'I refuse to trust someone who isn't interested in money!'

O raised her glass for a toast. 'To your principles, Henri.'

The businessman did not lose his temper. He knew from experience that if you attacked, and kept on attacking, a hundred times if necessary, you eventually achieved your objective. Attrition is one means to defeat strength. 'So: it isn't money. What then? Love?'

O shook her head. Carel pushed on. 'Hatred?'

O made the same reply. Carel was almost shouting now: 'So it's revenge?'

Once again O shook her head. Botterweg looked on with amusement; the two players were not disappointing him.

Carel seized O's wrist, pressing his nails into her delicate skin. 'So what is it then? Tell me!'

O pulled away, and watched the thin white indentations fade from her flesh. She sighed. 'I am a woman, Henri. And I am alive. Don't smile; the fact that I am still living does not prove to me that I am actually alive. The two words are very similar, but they mean different things. Some years ago I was living in total dependence on a man, out of love for him. It was a dependence that amounted to slavery; this man did whatever he wanted with me. If he had wished it, I would have obeyed him to the death. Now I am alive; my life is my own, and I know exactly what it is worth. I am free of desires, dreams, wishes. You are right to assume that I have agreed to take part in this business of yours for my own purposes. They concern no-one but me, and I cannot succeed unless they remain secret. This sounds very serious, doesn't it? But it has all become something of a game — a game that I happen to play to the bitter end. Or perhaps it is more like a hunt in which my quarry cannot escape his eventual fate. I'll explain the rules of the game — after I've won. But don't worry, Henri Carel: we are not competitors. We feed on different flesh.'

Carel pushed back his chair angrily. The waitress approached, but he waved her away with a scowl. He stood up and looked down at Botterweg. 'Daniel. It's impossible for me to predict how this situation will develop. We have absolutely no control over events. And it's all your fault. It was you who introduced O. Well, now it's up to you to sort the mess out. And I don't want to know how you do it.'

He turned to O, grabbed her hand and planted an angry kiss on it. 'And you, my little friend, should consider yourself lucky that I have a sense of humour. That's all that saved your chum Botterweg from dismissal after our little scene in the lift.'

O withdrew her hand as if she found the touch of Carel's

66

lips unpleasant. 'Humour,' she said, 'is a spontaneous emotion that occurs at the moment when something amusing happens. At any time after that, it is merely a pretext for other forms of behaviour.'

That was the last straw for Henri Carel. This woman, he decided, was unbearable. He still desired her, but his lust was mixed with anger and disdain. He wanted to possess O, to humiliate her, to beat her, to make her suffer until she screamed that she couldn't take any more; but at the same time he yearned to take her in his arms, to caress her; and beyond that he felt a need to offer himself to her as a devoted servant, ready to obey her in the way that she had been ready to obey her lover, eager to satisy her slightest whim. He realised that within him there was a slave who had no desire but to serve and obey, and the realisation filled him with disgust. He had to get out.

Before leaving the restaurant, he forced himself to address O once more. 'Please forgive me for cutting short this evening's meeting.'

'It has been delightful,' O said. 'Thank you.'

'The pleasure was entirely mine,' Carel said through gritted teeth.

'As it was last time, Monsieur Carel.'

Daniel Botterweg drew on a Havana cigar. The restaurant was now almost deserted; only the waitress in the blue kimono remained, silent and discreetly attentive. O asked her companion: 'Daniel, don't tell me you're doing all this to undermine Carel?'

'Of course not!' Botterweg protested. He watched a cloud of smoke make its way towards the ceiling, and added: 'But I must say that, since this evening, I've started to ask myself a few questions . . . '

O toyed with the iron ring that encircled her finger. She had lost weight over the years. 'Whatever I may do,

Botterweg, remember that it's not for you, or because of you, or for your benefit.'

Botterweg took her hand and kissed the ring of iron and gold. 'I understand,' he said. 'I've visited Roissy. Tell me, O, have you undertaken this task for Sir Stephen?'

O detached her hand from his. The question remained hanging in the air between them, and Botterweg regretted having asked it. It had been an error. He grabbed the jar on the table. '*Sake?*'

'If you like,' O replied.

9

The fashion show was held in the private rooms of a restaurant beside the Seine that had been famous at the beginning of the century. The exuberant frescoes, the pillars decorated with painted plasterwork, the glass vaulting and the Arabian ornaments still attracted those who were nostalgic for a time when beauty could be completely non-functional. Amongst the plaster women whose roseate flesh and hair of red and gold decorated the walls there now sauntered creatures that were only a little more animated. These were the models, strange beings of indeterminate gender, who were there to display the styles created by the *couturiers* – who on this occasion seemed to be promoting the imprisonment of the body in bizarre and painful costumes.

The models were wandering in the midst of an audience which was more intrigued by the docile mannequins, who were ready to adopt any pose on demand, than by the clothes they were wearing. Many of the spectators spared scarcely a glance for the entrance of a girl with green hair and impossibly high heels and pointed breasts encircled with metal. She was modelling a sort of brassiere with metallic cups in the shape of funnels. Only the tips of her breasts, coloured purple, were visible. Sally, who was drinking champagne with O and Jane, spotted this creation and could not restrain a gasp of surprise. 'It sure is lucky that James couldn't come with us. He'd think all this was positively indecent.'

'And you don't?' O asked; but at that moment Jane got up from the table.

'I want another glass of champagne,' the girl said. 'I'll go find Larry and make him get me one.'

As Jane made her way through the crowd she felt O's eyes following her, and she carefully exaggerated the swaying of her hips and arse. She found her brother standing at the edge of the hall, hardly daring to move in his stiff white tuxedo.

At the table Sally, as if accepting a challenge, was saying: 'Indecent, yes; but also exciting!'

'You are right, Sally,' said O. 'Propriety is often so boring.'

'Monotonous, that's for sure,' the American woman concluded, and then changed the subject: 'How come you know so much about this fashion scene?'

'I used to be a part of it, not so long ago. I was a photographer, in the fashion department of an agency. Nothing seems to have changed.'

Sally watched the models in silence. Not all the girls were pretty; some of them were exotic, wild and strange. The men were more predictably good-looking: each was either a Latin Lover, with smooth black hair and a pouting lower lip, or a Scandinavian Athlete, with steel-blue eyes and a shock of golden hair. O, Sally saw, was gazing almost wistfully at a model who had just entered the room: a slight girl with an entrancing smile and short blonde hair, who was wearing a vast dress of heavy red silk. The outfit was what the *couturiers* call a gala dress, designed to impress rather than to be worn; its *decolletage* was precariously low, and by contrast the voluminous skirt spread out from the tight waist like a tent. The matching shoes were of red silk with very high heels. 'O,' Sally said, 'that girl – do you know her?'

'No, I don't think so,' O sighed. 'But she looks like Jacqueline – a friend of mine who was a model. Do you like the dress?'

'It's fantastic, O. I just adore that gown. But who on earth could wear such a thing, apart from a young girl like that?'

70

O made no reply. She watched the model as she moved imperturbably between two rows of admirers and then out of the hall, on her way back to the dressing-room. O spoke in a far-away voice, and Sally was not sure whether she was intended to hear. 'I can picture the scene back there. All the girls, hurriedly undressing, touching up the make-up on their faces and their bodies, giving each other a quick embrace before struggling into the next outfit. Sometimes they caress each other as part of the show, of course: perhaps a Swedish girl and a Brazilian, for the effect of their contrasting skins. The audience is moved by it, but not the girls. They have already become part of other peoples's dreams.'

Sally decided that O was not seeking any response, and returned to the red silk dress. 'But you know James,' she laughed. 'Can you imagine, if I turned up to dinner wearing a dress like that? He'd kill me!'

'Then wear it for someone else,' said O. Sally wondered whether this was the Frenchwomans's idea of a joke; but O's eyes showed nothing but their usual clear emerald inscrutability.

'Another man?' Sally whispered.

'Do you have many?'

Sally shook her head slowly. 'For the life of me I don't know why, O, but I feel I can trust you. But James is always saying we have to be real cautious with strangers.'

'Perhaps he is right,' O said. 'But you and I are no longer strangers.'

'Hey, that's true. And anyway, I don't want to keep secrets from you. So yes, there have been some other men. That's inevitable, I guess. But I met them in the same circle, if you know what I mean. They were in business too. Let's face it, you could hardly tell them apart. That's why I've stuck where I am. If I left James I'd only wind up with another one that's not as good. You don't switch a Cartier

71

watch in case you get a rolled gold imitation in return.'

'That depends on what you want a watch for. As long as you're looking for style rather than durability, you can have a lot of fun with tat.'

Sally was looking at a pair of models. The girl was wearing a tunic that had been artfully torn to reveal her brown and naked body. She had china-blue eyes and long black hair in tight African-style plaits. The man behind her was wearing a black satin suit, wide across the shoulders and tight-fitting elsewhere. He looked exactly like a gigolo out to make money by promising his favours to a rich widow in a Mediterranean casino. He was holding the girl so tightly that they could move only by walking in unison. Their steps, their gestures and expressions, were almost parodically artificial, like an imitiation of the mating rituals of a couple of giant birds.

'Now that, I wouldn't be able to resist,' Sally said.

'The outfit, or the model?' O enquired innocently.

'The outfit, of course.'

'And why not the young man?'

'I'm prepared to let my imagination run a little wild,' Sally said, 'but that's all!'

'Perhaps you want to be forced?'

'Can we change the subject, please? When you get right down to it, I'm just like my husband. I don't like to joke about that sort of thing.'

A tall, slim man with grey hair came to their table. He had a moustache that was surprisingly blonde, and a sardonic smile. His pale eyes surveyed O and then Sally Pembroke. O greeted him and introduced him to Sally as Sir Stephen H. He gave an abbreviated bow and asked Sally whether she was enjoying the show.

'You're interested in fashion?' Sally replied. 'My husband wouldn't come with me to a thing like this for anything in the world.'

'I don't come for the fashion,' said Sir Stephen. 'What I like are the attendant rituals. I appreciate the ceremonial aspects of a show like this.' And he strolled away to a nearby table at which seats had been reserved for him.

Larry and Jane returned to their mother's table. Larry's face was flushed, from the heat of the room, or because he was excited, or as a result of drinking a little too much champagne.

'Come and sit down,' Sally said. 'You kids are taking no notice of the show.'

'Sit down?' said Larry, apparently confused. 'Sure, I could do with a rest. But where, Mom? There's not enough chairs for all of us.'

O took his arm and pointed to Sir Stephen sitting alone at his table. 'You see that man? He is a friend of mine. He'll be delighted to have you.'

Larry protested. 'But look, we don't know the guy.'

'Don't worry. He knows you. Go on.'

The young brother and sister approached Sir Stephen's table. The tall Englishman stood up, silent but wearing his usual slight smile. He indicated a seat for Larry, and for Jane he pulled up a chair which he placed alongside his own. Jane was tired and a little tipsy, and without thinking she fell into the chair with a sigh of exhaustion. Sir Stephen surveyed her for several minutes before he spoke. 'It seems, Jane, that you have already forgotten the correct way to sit.'

Jane was too confused to understand the import of his words. She tried to question him with an appealing look, but his grey eyes were as enigmatic as O's emerald gaze. And O, as far as Jane could tell, remained completely oblivious to Sir Stephen and was continuing her conversation with Jane's mother.

Very carefully, Jane lifted her backside from the upholstery and slid her skirt upwards. She lowered herself again, feeling Sir Stephen's look upon her as clearly as she

73

felt the velvet pile against her naked skin. At first she was nervous: it was clear to her that Sir Stephen had discovered the secret that she shared with O. And then it occurred to her that he was O's friend, and for some reason that calmed her. It seemed natural that he would know that she was bound to obey O's every instruction; that she was naked under her skirt. She shifted on the velvet seat, and smiled happily as the soft filaments tickled the tender places between her buttocks.

Sally Pembroke, meanwhile, was pointing to her son and daughter who were seated on either side of Sir Stephen. 'Look, I've two grown-up children,' she was saying, 'can you imagine me with a lover? I'd look ridiculous.'

'But my dear Sally,' O replied, 'if you don't take a lover today, tomorrow you may have to make do with a gigolo.'

'A gigolo? You mean, paid help? Well, that's not altogether an unattractive concept.'

'It depends on what you're looking for,' O said.

'How come?'

'It depends on whether you want love. Or sex.'

Sally replied withiout hesitation. 'Well, it isn't love, that's for sure.'

'Then you are looking for sex?'

'O, honey, how can you ask me a question like that? These aren't the kind of things you talk about.'

'But they are the things that one does.'

'That's easier than talking, maybe. You know, I think I will have that red gown after all. What the hell — James doesn't know the first thing about clothes. And he doesn't ask me for advice about crude oil prices.'

O gave her an approving smile. Then she pointed out that the satin-suited male model had re-entered the hall and was now wandering among the tables as in search of someone. O beckoned to him.

'Karl,' she said as the young man approached, 'Madame Pembroke would like to meet you. She thought your performance was very impressive.'

The man smiled, revealing two golden incisors among otherwise very white teeth. His bearing and expression were those of a refined and civilised gentleman; but his outward appearance could not conceal an elemental savagery. Sally realised instinctively that he was a dangerous creature. And she knew almost as quickly that this was what appealed to her.

'I'm afraid I'm not as young as that gorgeous partner of yours just now,' Sally simpered. 'Surely a wild outfit like that, on me, would make men run away?'

'Not at all,' Karl replied, 'you would attract men, irresistibly. Women who are in love with love are the most seductive for we unfortunate men.'

'So you think I'm in love with love, Karl?'

'I do not think it. I know it.'

During the silence that followed, O stood up and offered her seat to the young man. 'I can already see,' she said to Sally, 'that you two have a great deal to talk about.'

Sally could not prevent her from leaving; and in any case Karl had already taken her hand and gave no indication that he was going to let go of it. It felt very pleasant. She abandoned herself to his gentle touch.

Larry could not take his eyes off the girl. She had red hair and freckles across her bare shoulders; she was tall and slim, and wearing a black sheath-dress that cinched her waist and supported her bosom like a shelf.

When he had first seen her, at the moment she had entered the hall, Larry had been overwhelmed by the same feelings he had experienced, in the chateau, before the statue of Diana. He was in the grip of an emotion that went beyond ordinary desire: he felt that with this woman he could be taken beyond his conscious fantasies, that he could be made to explore his most deep-seated longings.

It seemed that nothing escaped the attention of Sir Stephen; and as the red-head passed the table he looked at her and raised an eyebrow. The girl paused, and as if by accident Larry let his hand trail across the sheath-dress where it constrained her thigh. The young woman looked down at him, her head lowered and her lips slightly parted.

Larry felt his heart leaping in his chest. He would have liked to ask the girl to sit beside him, to dazzle her and make her laugh with brilliant and witty conversation, and then to take her back to the chateau knowing that she was completely his. But he knew nothing like that would happen. He knew he was just a dumb Yankee, that he would not be able to find the right words, that he was more at home on a baseball pitch than across a table from a pretty girl. With some bitterness he reflected that his father, with his millions, could simply buy this red-head, at least for a time; but he knew that he was incapable of finding the few words that would seduce her. These things are not taught in American schoolrooms, although they are more useful than knowing the date of George Washington's birthday or the laws of thermodynamics.

As if by chance, Sir Stephen came to the rescue. He indicated to the young woman that she should take a seat at the next table. 'Karen,' he said, 'you look more delicious than ever. I'm sure you'd like a rest and a glass of champagne. Stay here while Larry fetches one for you.'

Larry's jaw dropped in amazement; and then he jumped to his feet. Terrified that the colour rising in his cheeks might betray his feelings, he muttered: 'Uh – yeah – of course – no problem – ' and disappeared into the crowd.

Jane looked for O, and was disappointed that she couldn't see her beautiful friend. She saw her mother, apparently rapt in conversation with a tall young man; and then turned her

76

attention to Karen. The red-head's black dress was very tight-fitting, but Jane saw that as she had sat down she had managed to slide the material up her legs and was now sitting with her thighs uncovered and slightly parted. The black dress was bunched round her tiny waist and scarcely covered her hips. Jane realised that, like hers, Karen's naked sex was resting on cushioned velvet.

Larry returned with a tray, glasses, and a bottle. He poured several glasses, and took one to Karen who immediately raised it to her lips. 'I really need this!' she said.

'Me too,' Jane said to her, taking a glass from the tray. 'That's another thing that you and I have in common.'

Jane saw O at last, chatting to a group of men who were simultaneously flirtatious and respectful. Jane wondered whether O had made love with all of them, but then decided that the answer was irrelevant. The Englishman was getting on her nerves; his grey eyes missed none of her words, expressions and gestures. She felt that she was being studied like an animal in a zoo.

He should know all about me, Jane thought, the way he's been staring at me. She wondered whether he had noticed her full and rounded lower lip; this was a sure sign of sensuality, as Jane had been told by her schoolfriend Marcia. And then, without warning, Marcia had glued her mouth to Jane's, biting and sucking that inviting lower lip. Jane had let it happen, astonished to find that this unwanted kiss, from a girl to whom she felt no attraction, could give her so much pleasure.

Has Sir Stephen seen the scar on the side of my nose, she wondered. The barely-detectable white line was a souvenir of a fall from a bicycle: she had been fleeing from her brother, who had wanted her to show him the places where she was different from him. Until that day she had consented to play these games; in fact she rather liked handling her brother's little willy and watching it grow stiff and red. On this occasion she had refused, and Larry had tried to make her. She had escaped on Larry's bicycle, which was too big for her, and had fallen off at the first bend in the track. She was bleeding copiously when rescued. She still enjoyed her recollections of the servants' panic, the sobbing of her brother (who was feeling guilty and who was always given plenty of consolation because of his sensitive nature), the smell of ether, and her father's warm embrace as he held her on knees while the doctor stitched the wound.

Trying to deflect Sir Stephen's gaze, she said: 'O seems to have lots of friends.'

'I am pleased that you have noticed,' Sir Stephen said, without looking away from her.

Jane fidgeted. 'Well, I guess I should be going home now,' she suggested.

Larry threw her an anxious glance. He didn't want to have to accompany his sister just as Karen seemed to be showing some interest in him — or at least she listened to him, and smiled, and sometimes spoke.

'You're not going home,' Sir Stephen said.

'Who's going to stop me?' she demanded, with a defiance that she already guessed would be futile.

'Why, nobody,' Sir Stephen said.

'What do you mean?'

'You have no need of explanations. You have only to obey.'

Jane saw that O was approaching the table, and she gave O an imploring look, a mute appeal for help. O made no response, in fact gave no indication that she had noticed her young friend's distress; and Jane felt a wave of panic sweep over her. She told herself that the whole thing was crazy: all she had to do was to stand up and say good-bye, as she had done in similar circumstances all through her life, and the scene would be over. But she no longer had the power to do it. Her will had been destroyed. She was appalled to find nothing within her except submission. In a dry voice, Sir Stephen said: 'Lower your eyes, Jane.'

The girl did not want to surrender. She told herself that there was no reason why she should obey this unknown Englishman. Even now she thought of rebelling, but then she was aware of someone standing behind her, and she heard O's soft and persuasive voice. 'Do as he says.'

'But why?'

'Do you remember our conversation? Do you recall what I told you next to the tennis courts?'

'You said I must be ready,' Jane said.

'And that I would come for you when you least expect it,' O added. 'That time has arrived.'

'Now?'

'Now.'

'But — '

'But what?' O asked.

Sir Stephen followed this exchange as if it were a discussion about the cost of a dress. Jane had almost said: 'Because I'm not ready!', but she knew it was an unacceptable excuse, and that to utter it would lose her O's love. So she stood up, and waited with the deference that she knew was expected of her.

'Go now,' O said to her, 'and obey. You are strong, and the strong obey best.'

Sir Stephen stood, and strode towards the exit. Jane hesitated and then, at a sign from O, followed him. As she passed O she heard the Frenchwoman whisper: 'Don't worry. I'll be there.'

Jane made for the exit. A man of about thirty, in a grey suit, followed her.

10

A black Daimler was waiting beside the pavement. The chauffeur, in a white uniform and a peaked cap, remained at the wheel when Sir Stephen and Jane appeared. The Englishman opened the door himself and indicated that Jane should enter the vehicle; he followed her. They were joined by the grey-suited young man, who went to the other side of the limousine before getting in, so that Jane found herself sitting between the two men. She had remembered to raise the back of her skirt, and the touch of the cold leather seat caused her to shiver. She felt like a prisoner, or a hostage who had just been kidnapped and was about to be taken into hiding. She would have welcomed some indication that she had no reason to be afraid; but when she looked towards the Englishman's sharp profile, with its thin moustache and cruel eye, she was seized with a terror that clenched her thighs and froze her stomach.

A glass panel, such as one finds in British taxi-cabs, separated the rear seats from the chauffeur. Sir Stephen gave one brisk tap on the glass and, without acknowledging the instruction, the chauffeur shifted the transmission lever and the car glided away.

Jane had no idea where they were going; she had no way of recognising the different *quartiers* through which they drove. They were, in fact, heading towards the outskirts of Paris: they passed the tower-blocks of La Defense and then joined the *peripherique*. The traffic was sparse and the Daimler sped along smoothly. They took the *autoroute du Nord*, and at the slip-road Jane had time to make out a road-sign that read: *Aeroport Roissy-Charles de Gaulle*.

She began to wonder whether she was the victim of a real kidnapping. Perhaps she had been wrong to trust O. She had heard stories about girls who disappeared, never to be seen again, and who were sold into enforced prostitution in exotic countries. She could not hold back a fearful sob. Sir Stephen slowly turned his head to look at her. 'You must not cross your legs. Neither are you to press them together.'

Automatically, Jane obeyed, separating her legs so that they did not touch each other at any point. In the same impassive voice Sir Stephen said: 'Now keep still. Don't move an inch.'

He drew a penknife from his pocket and leant towards her. Jane recoiled from him, but only as far as the young man in grey, who was still staring straight ahead and seemed oblivious to her. 'What do you want?' she begged.

'You must remain silent,' was Sir Stephen's only reply. 'Don't say a word.'

His voice restored some small element of normality to the scene, and Jane kept quiet and motionless as he unbuttoned her blouse. He reached beneath the material to cut the straps of Jane's brassiere and remove it. Her blouse hung open, and beneath it her breasts were naked; and in the same way the friction of the leather against her buttocks and her sex reminded her that she was naked under her skirt. She was fully clothed, but she had never felt more exposed. Sir Stephen was holding a blindfold. 'Put this over your eyes,' he said.

Without a word Jane complied. As she finished tying the band behind her blonde hair, she felt the young man move for the first time. There was a mechanical noise that Jane recognised as the sound of an audio cassette being loaded; and then O's voice, soft and husky, filled the car. Jane listened attentively.

'Jane, I promised that one day I would tell you about my experiences – my apprenticeship. Now is the time. Listen carefully to me. You are going to relive my past as if you were me. I mean by this not only that you will hear my story, but also that you will re-live it. As I tell my story it will, little by little and step by step, become your reality. My story will soon be yours . . . '

Jane's throat was dry. She thought she would suffocate for lack of air. Being unable to see was unbearable. But then the recorded voice of the woman she trusted as her guide continued. 'It was in the autumn, late one afternoon. My lover, Rene, had taken me for a walk in the park. On a street corner there was a taxi rank. There was only one taxi waiting there; it was similar to the car you are in today.'

O's voice took on a more serious tone, and Jane trembled. 'As you have no lover, Jane, and have never had one, I will play the part of your lover. I will be your guide, as Rene was mine. Listen closely to what I am about to say: you are free to go if you want to. You have only to remove the blindfold, and everything will stop at once. But if you don't stop now, from this moment on you will not be able to turn back. Events will take their course and you will be unable to do anything to affect them.'

Jane heard a click as the cassette player was switched off; and then nothing but the breathing of the two men, barely perceptible above the whispering of the Daimler's engine. She put a hand to the blindfold; touched the material; and, with a feeling of great sadness, let her hand fall again. She clenched her fist and resumed her position: sitting very straight, with her legs apart and her hands resting on her thighs.

There was another click, and O's voice restarted. 'We arrived in a grand avenue lined with plane trees. The car stopped in front of a small mansion. It was raining. Rene said to me: "You are ready now. I'm leaving you here. Get out of the car and go and ring the bell. You are to go with whoever opens the door, and do whatever you are instructed to do. If you don't go in straight away, you will be hunted down; if you don't obey orders willingly and promptly, you will be forced to obey." '

At that moment Jane sensed that the car was moving to one side, slowing down, and stopping. A door opened and the young man took Jane's arm to help her leave the car. She heard O's final words: 'He said to me: "You are just a woman that I am supplying. Yes, I'll be there. Now go!" '

Jane left the car and shivered as if she were naked and it was the middle of the night. The young man and Sir Stephen guided her up a few steps and through two doors. Sir Stephen removed the blindfold and left her alone in a dark room.

There was no light and no sound. Jane tried to orient herself but gave up in despair, frustrated by the absolute blackness of the room and the absence of any features that she could feel on the walls. She started counting the seconds in an attempt to calculate how much time was passing, but became confused and abandoned the attempt. She thought about O, and wondered where she was. O's taped voice was a negligible comfort, really, and had done almost nothing to alleviate the strange and oppressive presence of the two men in the car; but Jane longed to hear those familiar tones, just as a sailor searches the skies for a clear view of Polaris.

A turmoil of thoughts and sensations swirled through her mind. She hated being held prisoner in the dark, but she had to admit that she did not want to be rescued — not for anything in the world.

She heard a door opening, and at the same time O's voice: 'I was left for an hour or two, I don't know how long it was, but it felt like a century . . . '

A light was switched on. Jane averted her eyes from the glare, but saw that she was in a room that was, as she had thought, devoid of furniture. The only decoration was the thick carpet on the floor. Two women were facing her; they

were young and pretty. They wore flaring skirts above which
their waists were tightly corseted; their outthrust breasts were
supported, but not covered, by the corsets they wore. Jane
saw that the two women were heavily made up: their eyes
were outlined in black, their eyelids were a brilliant shade
of green, and their lips were dark purple. Each wore a collar
around her neck and a bracelet around each wrist.

They told told Jane that she was to undress. As she was
wearing very little, this was quickly achieved. One of the
women took her blouse, skirt and shoes and opened a door
in the wall; Jane realised that the room was surrounded by
walk-in wardrobes. Her clothes were put away and she was
led from the room.

The two women took her to another chamber in which
every surface — ceiling as well as walls — was covered with
mirrors. Wherever she was Jane could not escape the sight
of her own naked body being manipulated and prepared by
the two women. The room was furnished rather like a
bathroom, and indeed Jane's preparation started with a
bath. As they soaped and rinsed every part of Jane's body
the women exchanged a few brief sentences. They spoke in
French, and although Jane understood most of the words
they said, she made no contribution to the conversation. In
any case they said nothing that told Jane where she was;
their comments were almost all merely expressions of
approval of Jane's physiognimy — 'What lovely golden
hair!' and 'The sun-tan really is all over, see?' and 'A very
cute little arse! They'll love that.' Some of the things they
said made Jane shiver with a mixture of excitement and
dread; in particular one of the women, having patted Jane
dry with a soft warm towel, was idly stroking the girl's
breasts and said: 'Such pretty things. Small and firm — and
such clear skin. They won't remain unmarked for long. But
perhaps they will look even prettier . . . ' And the other
woman had replied: 'They will think so, anyway. They

always do. And they'll use the riding-crop, you can bet on it. The crop is only good for big girls like you, *cherie*; they should use the whip on this one.' It was not only the words that unnerved Jane; even more disturbing was the fact that the women conversed in hurried whispers, as if afraid of retribution if overheard.

After the bath pungent oils were massaged into Jane's skin. The fragrances were earthy and bitter, redolent of ferns and animal furs. Once again the women paid prolonged attention to certain areas of Jane's body: her neck and shoulders, the small of her back, her armpits, as might be expected; but also her breasts, the insides of her thighs and, above all, the delicate furrow between her buttocks.

By now languorous and sensual, Jane was next taken to sit in a large chair such as one finds in a hairdressing salon; and, indeed, the women tilted the chair backwards and started to dress Jane's blonde tresses. The girl gazed upwards at the ceiling and was momentarily nonplussed to see herself, reflected in a huge mirror, with her thighs spread apart and her head back as if offering herself to the world. She thought of moving her legs together, but one of the women detected the movement and gently eased the girl's thighs back to the sides of the chair.

More than an hour had passed in the mirrored room. The women worked in silence now – perhaps, Jane thought, because there was no longer the sound of flowing water to drown their whispered asides. They had soft hands and treated Jane very gently, with as much skill as the *coiffeuse* and manicurist of an expensive beauty salon. Having brushed perfumed conditioner into Jane's hair, they used turquoise slides and a few pins to create a simple style that swept her hair away from her forehead and accentuated the pointed oval of her face. Then they moved on to painting her fingernails and toenails; and then they used fine brushes to apply the various stages of make-up to her face. Jane

85

abandoned herself to their attentions; only her gaping nudity, which she could not avoid glimpsing in the mirrors, reminded her of the strangeness of her situation.

Crimson lipstick was applied to her lips; a slightly lighter colour was used for her nipples and her labia. Finally, the women decided that Jane's golden fleece of pubic hair was too profuse, and they shaved her; she was left with a small triangle of curls which they seemed to think formed a much better setting for the pink slit of her sex.

Although the two women had not told anyone that they had finished preparing Jane, a man entered the room. He was wearing a long purple robe, with wide sleeves that narrowed at the wrists, which fell open as he walked. The first thing that Jane noticed was that he was naked under the robe: her eyes were drawn to his dangling member, long, thin and dark.

This was not the first time that Jane had seen a male organ. In fact while she was still at high school she had sometimes gone so far as to touch and fondle the hard vibrating rod of a boyfriend, late at night when both he and she had had a little too much to drink; once or twice, impelled by the urgent pleas that the boy would gasp in the brief moments that his lips separated from hers, she had continued to manipulate the hot and tortured flesh until the boy groaned and warm liquid spurted into her hand. Even earlier than this, of course, she had seen her brother. Larry was without shame in front of his sister: he undressed in her presence and seemed to delight in exhibiting his sexual parts to her as often as he could. But none of these adolescent experiences had prepared her for this; and it seemed to her that the deliberately exposed penis of the robed man was peculiarly threatening.

He spoke to her in a tone that implied that he expected nothing from her but obedience. 'Come with me!' was all he said.

86

It was only then that Jane noticed the whip, made of several strips of leather, that was hanging from his belt, and the black cowl that covered his head. His face was masked, and even his eyes were hidden, veiled with fine black tulle.

He led her into another room, empty apart from a pouffe in the middle of the floor. Again, the walls were entirely covered with mirrors. The two women followed Jane, and the masked man asked them whether they had taken the girl's measurements. They replied that they had not had time. 'Hurry up, then!' he barked.

Using a dressmaker's tape measure the women measured Jane's wrists and neck. Then one of them opened the mirrored door of a wall-cupboard, produced a basket containing an assortment of bracelets and collars, and selected several items of the correct size for Jane. All were of the same type: bands of leather, no thicker than a finger, each with a metal fastening that, like a padlock, clicked shut but could be re-opened only with a key. Jane noticed that set at regular intervals into the outer circumference of each band were metal rings with slip-catches; as the bracelets and collar closed around her wrists and neck, just a little too tightly to be completely comfortable, she felt a resurgence of panic as she imagined how the rings could be used to pinion her body into any number of helpless positions. She could not shake from her mind the memory of the wax prisoners in the dungeons at Madame Tussaud's, which she visited while in London the previous year.

'She's ready now,' said one of the women; and the man seized Jane's arms, pulled them together behind her back, and joined the bracelets together with a click. Jane felt her legs almost give way beneath her. The women placed a red cloak round her shoulders.

'Go on!' the man ordered; and Jane stumbled forward. The cloak covered her completely but opened with each step that she took; and with her hands secured behind her back she was powerless to prevent this involuntary exposure of her projecting, pink-tipped breasts and her carefully-prepared pudenda.

They proceeded through a series of rooms and corridors. One of the women went ahead to open the doors; the other brought up the rear and closed the doors again. The man walked alongside Jane in silence. With each step that took her nearer to her unknown destination Jane felt more naked, more powerless, more vulnerable, more filled with foreboding, and more aware of the sacrificial exhibition of her body.

They arrived at a set of double doors. The man stood aside. 'Go on,' he said, and left. The two women stood on either side of Jane and opened the doors to reveal a library. They walked in side by side.

A pile of logs blazed in the fireplace. Four men were sitting in leather armchairs and drinking coffee. They wore purple robes, but were not masked. Jane recognised two of them: Sir Stephen and the young man who had sat next to her in the Daimler. Sir Stephen waved the two women from the room; Jane was left alone, naked and fettered beneath her red cloak, transfixed by the unwavering looks of the men, who, silent and unmoving, watched her embarassment as they sipped their drinks.

At last the young man stood up, strolled over to her, and pushed her towards the fireplace, to within reach of all of the men. One of them removed her cloak. Another stroked her buttocks and, when she twisted away from him, he turned his attention to her breasts while the third man teased her pubic hair and parted her lower lips. Jane began to whimper in terror; but Sir Stephen, from his chair, merely said: 'Turn her round. I want to see her breasts and her belly.'

Jane was turned to face him. She caught a glimpse of his grey eyes calmly surveying her, and then her head was forced forward so that one of the men could check the fit of her collar; but she knew he was watching her, watching every expression that crossed her face as the cheeks of her arse were kneaded, slapped, and pulled apart; as a finger twisted its way into her arsehole; as one breast was squeezed in a hand while the tip of the other was enveloped by a warm mouth. Occasionally one or other of the men would speak, commenting on some intimate part of her body in the crudest of terms.

'Make her kneel,' the young man said, and Jane was pushed to her knees and held with her legs spread apart and her buttocks resting on her heels.

'I want to see her cunt,' said another of the men; and Jane was tilted backwards. She stared up at the beams that crossed the ceiling as she felt her thighs being pulled wider apart. One of the men supported her shoulders and rolled one of her nipples between a finger and thumb while the others inspected her sex. Jane felt pain in the muscles of her thighs and in the small of her back, but the men did not hurt her as they pulled at the rouged folds of skin and probed her secret recesses.

Sir Stephen ordered her to be tied to a pillar in the room, so that she would be on display to everyone, available for everyone to peruse and touch. But one of the men protested: 'She's gorgeous. We can't wait. We want to have her straight away.'

On hearing this Jane was once again overwhelmed by an attack of panic. She opened her mouth to scream; or at least to object; but the words died in her throat. She had, after all, decided to stay; she had known in advance that any show of defiance would be useless. She had agreed to abide by the rules of the game as laid down by O. She had not left when she still had time to leave; and now she had to accept her fate.

In any case she knew in her heart that even her resistance was just one more gambit in the game that she had already consented to play. As she had entered the Daimler with Sir Stephen she had foreseen that she was setting off on a journey of initiation from which she would not return unchanged. This was what she had asked of O; and O would keep her word. In spite of everything, Jane felt an excitement, an anticipation of what was to come. She feared it but she longed for it, to the extent that she was impatient with the slow pace of the proceedings; but she guessed that the protraction of her sacrifice was as much a part of the ritual as the bizarre surroundings, the meticulous preparation of her body, and the ceremonial dressing and undressing.

The young man was the first to penetrate her. She was turned to stand in front of him; he put his hands on her hips and, as she was lowered slowly to the floor, he moved his hands to her thighs, separating them so that he came to rest between her legs, his robe spreading like a tent over both his body and hers, his red member trembling at the entrance of Jane's sex like a gigantic humming-bird hovering before an exotic bloom. Jane froze; and then, as a shy teenager lifts her face for a first kiss, she offered her lower mouth to the man's waiting organ.

The young man began to move. At first, he used the tip of his penis to stroke her gently, following the rouged lines of her outer labia before pressing between them, turning them aside, and pushing slowly and carefully into the secret folds within.

Jane started to breathe faster and more deeply; she could hear her own heartbeat. As the young man's member, so stiff and yet so soft, roved back and forth between the exquisitely sensitive apex of her slit and the aching sweetness at the entrance to her womb, it seemed to Jane that her lower body had a life of its own, independent of her conscious control. She told herself she was frightened; she told herself she was detached, uninvolved; and yet her private parts were bathed in her own wetness. Then the man lowered his body on to hers, and slowly thrust his way into her. Inexorably he penetrated her; as he tore her maidenhead she screamed.

He stopped only when he could go no further; every centimetre of his cock was buried inside her, its tip had reached the neck of her cervix. Jane was aware of nothing but the burning heat that filled her belly; all the same, her flesh contracted around the man's shaft. He started to move up and down, each movement adding to her pain; there was just the man on top of her, the burning mass deep within her, and the steady, relentless motion which, although it never ceased to hurt her, began to resonate with the surges of pleasure that shook her body.

The man was not interested in her enjoyment, however, but merely in his enjoyment of her. Without uttering a sound he released himself inside her; she hardly felt the spurts of hot liquid, feeling instead only a mixture of relief and disappointment as he withdrew.

A second man pulled her to her feet and entered her immediately, and Jane abandoned any final thoughts of resistance. She groaned, she pleaded, she cried out, she wept, aware of the clinically interested gazes of the onlookers, aware of nothing else but her bruised and ravished body. As she writhed and moaned against the unceasing thrusts, she saw with sudden clarity that her body was moving to another's rhythm, that her cries were for the benefit of her audience. She was, she realised, beginning to understand the happiness to be found in submission.

When the man left her, she slid to the floor. The third man knelt next to her, and she was lifted so that her breasts were crushed against his thighs. Fingers prised open her lips, and she knew that her mouth was not going to be spared. She made a circle of her lips to accommodate the rigid stem, and tasted a man for the first time. She licked and sucked the flesh that filled her mouth, but this was not enough for the man, who drove into the back of her throat, determined to use Jane's untutored mouth only for his own pleasure. The girl gagged and choked, and at last the man flooded her mouth with viscous jets of fluid that she had to swallow, sobbing with disgust.

The men watched her for a while. She was still lying on the carpet, crying, her make-up running down her face, when Sir Stephen stood up at last. He raised her to her knees and rested her head on a black velvet pouffe. With sharp slaps he made her part her legs, and he pushed down the small of her back so that her buttocks were thrust upwards and outwards. He spent some time on another inspection of her haunches and the cleft between them; and then with a single brutal thrust he forced his iron-hard member into her anal orifice. Jane's cry of surprise became a sobbing moan of pain. Sir Stephen pushed again, and Jane thought she would die from the violence of the assault. She lost track of how long the torture lasted; she even lost count of the waves of pain. The other men laughed and joked each time Sir Stephen pressed in and forced a gasp of agony from Jane's lips. With each lunge, the Englishman demanded to know whether the girl had started to cry; and although she tried to resist it, Jane could not in the end prevent the tears that coursed down her face — tears of pain, resentment, futile anger and helpless shame. And then Sir Stephen finished.

Jane rolled on to her side and stayed there, motionless, her face pressed into the soft pile of the carpet. She hardly heard the men leave the room.

She was still lying on the floor, aware of only the burning in her loins and between her legs and buttocks, the aching in the muscles of her legs and her pinioned arms, the pain of each ragged breath she drew into her lungs.

Something touched her wrist; her hands were freed; and

a gentle hand stroked her hair. She smelt the wild perfume that O wore; and she turned and threw herself into the young woman's waiting arms. O pushed her head back and kissed her on the lips. Jane pulled herself free and started to cry again, hot, comforting children's tears.

O sat beside her and stroked her face; and Jane surrendered to the tender attentions of her friend. O caressed her back and her thighs, and then trailed her fingers across the girl's stomach and towards her tingling sex. Jane tried to avoid this questing hand, but O made her keep her thighs apart. Then O turned and leant forward, gently parted the girl's tender lower lips with the tips of her fingers, and searched with the tip of her tongue for Jane's hidden nodule of flesh. She found it; licked it, twirled her tongue around it and, when it was erect and stiff, she held it between her lips and sucked it. Jane shut her eyes; with her body rigid, she waited for the explosion of pleasure that was gathering in her belly. She started to moan, softly at first, then more and more loudly; and at last she shrieked, a shout such as she had never before uttered, a cry that came from the very core of her being and that was not merely an expression of her climax but was a part of it.

Jane was absolutely exhausted. She wanted nothing but to go to sleep in O's arms. Instead, the masked man entered the library, pulled the whip from his belt and offered it to O. Jane was almost too tired to feel panicked. O seemed to be talking to herself rather than to Jane or the masked man. 'Your beautiful body,' she whispered, 'so young, so smooth. These tears on your face — which ones are the tears of pain, and which of joy? Your shining eyes, so full of every emotion . . . '

She told the masked man to leave, and said to Jane: 'There is more to this story. But we'll keep it for another chapter.'

11

Larry experienced a thrill of excitement at returning to the statue of Diana. He was pleasantly drunk – with champagne, of course, but he was even more inebriated by the presence of Karen at his side. He was clinging to her arm; she smiled ironically, but didn't shake him off. 'We've arrived,' she said. 'Surely you're not afraid of losing me now?'

'You just can't tell,' Larry replied. 'Most everyone else has disappeared this evening – Mom, and Jane – so I'm going to hold on to you.'

'What will you give me to stay?' laughed the girl.

'Champagne!'

'*Parfait*!' said the red-head. 'Let's go and find some.'

The model started towards the kitchen. Larry, perplexed, followed her. 'So you've been here before?'

'*Naturellement*.'

'What for?'

'Would you be jealous if I told you?'

Larry cursed himself for blushing like a schoolboy. These French women, he told himself, were something else. He just wasn't used to girls being so cheeky. The way they moved, the way they talked, just the way they smiled was enough to knock him sideways and make him as horny as a bull steer. None of which was conducive to witty small-talk.

Karen took his hand. 'Come on,' she said, 'don't get angry. You have better things to do tonight than to indulge in jealous little sulks.'

Karen's hand was as warm and soft as a kiss. She added,

conspiratorially: 'There are always a few bottles of chilled Dom Perignon in the kitchen — a useful custom, my dear Larry.'

They wandered along several corridors on their way to the kitchen. Larry was afraid they might meet his father: he would be home by that time of night, bombarding the world with threatening telephone calls — sell this! buy that! — as he ceaselessly augmented his fortune. For a moment Larry wondered whether his father had ever experienced the midnight enchantment of pursuing a supremely desirable woman, confident that she would soon give herself to him. Larry no longer had any doubt that Karen would — tonight — consent to be his.

'Here we are,' she said, and opened a wooden door to reveal a room with tiled walls. In the centre of the room was a rustic wooden table on which stood baskets of fruit and vegetables. Round the walls were cupboards and racks containing pots, pans, and all the hundreds of tools and containers that are required in a kitchen. Larry had never before seen so many different spices; and hanging from the ceiling were strings of garlic and bouquets of dried herbs. He gave an appreciative whistle: it was just a simple kitchen, but it contained more food and equipment than he'd seen in one place. The kitchen at home looked empty — shiny bare surfaces, anonymous units, and everything, including the freezer and the microwave, white and box-shaped. He began to understand why the food here in Europe had so much flavour, was almost overwhelmingly tasty. Would love be the same, he wondered. He wanted to ask the question out loud but thought Karen might laugh at him.

As if she had known the place all her life, the young woman opened a cupboard and brought out an ice-bucket containing a bottle of champagne. She placed it on the table, pulled out the bottle, and pushed her thumbs against the cork.

With a loud pop the cork flew from the bottle. A little foam bubbled from the neck and dripped to the floor, filling Larry's imagination with other images. To cover his embarassment, he blurted out: 'You've forgotten the glasses!'

Karen gave him a long look with her cool blue eyes, and smiled. 'We don't need glasses.'

'You want to drink out of the bottle? Sure, why not.'

Karen shook her head, her red hair swinging prettily. 'Use a little imagination, Larry.'

Larry was bewildered. He looked for something he could drink from. Karen came to his aid: 'Give me your hands.'

Larry held out his hands. She took them and put them together, as if he were a child at a drinking fountain. 'Press them together, like that, to make a bowl.'

'Like this?'

'That's better. Press tightly.'

Larry did as he was told. Karen took the bottle and poured champagne into his joined palms. The liquid bubbled over and dripped to the floor, and Larry burst out laughing. 'Now don't move!' Karen ordered.

Larry stopped in mid-guffaw, surprised by the young woman's sudden solemnity. She leant towards him, positioned her face above his hands, and with one last secretive look from her blue eyes she started to lap the remaining champagne, like a kitten lapping milk, from the hollows of his palms. Her tongue flickered across his hands, and then moved to linger lovingly at his wrists. Larry had never felt such indescribable sensations. There was something about this caress that made it more intimate than if the young woman had simply grabbed his penis. It was almost unbearable; and Larry had to push her away.

'Well what about me?' he exclaimed. 'Don't I get any champagne? You give me your hand now.'

'Ah no. You'll have to find something else.'

'Your shoe!'

'Take it.'

She lifted her foot towards Larry. The young man bent to remove the shoe, discovering at the same time that although her foot was clothed in fine silk, her legs were bare under the black sheath dress.

He stood up red-faced and excited, brandishing the shoe. It was a high-heeled style, sling-backed and open-toed. Larry did his best to joke about it: 'Not exactly purpose-built for drinking champagne out of!'

'What gave you the idea?' Karen asked.

'I saw it in a movie. It was set here, in Paris – at Maxim's, I think. There were Russian Grand Dukes and can-can dancers.'

'You needed to imagine the good life?' Karen said with some sarcasm.

'Gee, I was only fourteen! It just made me think that one day I'd like to do that, to drink champagne from the shoe of a beautiful woman.'

'It's a very touching story,' Karen said. 'We must find a solution. Childhood dreams should never be disappointed.'

She took her shoe and lifted it to Larry's face. 'Open your mouth!' she said, and Larry obeyed. She placed the toe of the shoe on his lower lip and poured a trickle of champagne into the shoe. Larry was able to swallow the first few mouthfuls, but he choked on the bubbles and his face was soon submerged in a sea of foam. The wine flowed down his chin and soaked his neck and his shirt.

'You lack training,' Karen laughed.

'You can train for this? Like for baseball?'

'Everything, Larry. Everything is a matter of training. This is something that is rarely stated, but it is very useful to know.'

Larry felt a sudden pang of anxiety. This woman was formidable. Much stronger than he was. Dangerous. He realised that perhaps it had not been a good idea to bring her here; he wondered how he could get rid of her before it was too late. But Karen had already changed the subject. She pressed a bell and said: 'I'm hungry.'

Natalie appeared at once, dressed in her maid's uniform, her face made up and her hair pinned back as if it were the middle of the day. 'Don't you ever sleep?' Larry said; but Natalie seemed to think the question unworthy of a reply.

'Make supper for us,' Karen instructed her; and without hesitation the maid produced smoked salmon from the refridgerator, and began to toast some brown bread.

Larry was amazed. 'You two know each other? You know Natalie?'

Karen grabbed Natalie by her waist, turned the maid to face her, and kissed her on the mouth. Larry saw Natalie open her lips and return Karen's kiss with equal ardour; then Karen pushed her away. 'No,' Karen said, 'I don't know her.'

'And if you did?' Larry said with a nervous laugh, 'That would be . . . '

'Less exciting,' Karen said.

Natalie had returned to putting out dishes for the meal. Larry felt that somehow he was missing something. Everything seemed perfectly natural but also as unreal as a dream. 'And what about me?' he burst out. 'What am I supposed to do in all this?'

'If you're hungry,' Karen said, 'you prepare something to eat. Or you get someone else to do it for you.'

They're making a monkey out of me, Larry thought. They're in it together. I've been suckered into some kind of trap − and I'll bet it's going to cost Dad plenty. I can already hear the sermons I'll get − and then it'll be straight back to College . . .

'Women are the same,' Karen was saying. 'If you want

a woman, Larry, you have to prepare her. Or have her prepared for you by someone else.'

'It's ready,' Natalie said in a strangely ambiguous tone. There was hot toast on the table, wine, cheeses, Beluga caviar, and smoked salmon. Natalie lit a match and lifted it to the candles in the chandelier. Karen switched off the electric lights; the remaining unsteady candlelight reminded Larry of the black masses that some of his schoolfriends had claimed to have attended.

'Good,' Karen said, and took Natalie by the hand. She led the maid to the table and made her sit on it, amidst the dishes and the baskets of fruit and vegetables.

Slowly, Karen unbuttoned the maid's black blouse, releasing two large, round, pale, blue-veined breasts. She turned to watch Larry's face as she grasped the breasts in her crimson-nailed hands, crushing them against her palms, twisting them with her fingers, scratching red lines across them with her nails. Natalie remained silent, but threw back her head and opened her legs. Karen lowered her head and took the maid's nipples between her teeth, nibbling, licking and sucking first one and then the other, leaving her victim's swollen points as red as her own swinging hair.

Then she pulled the maid forward, roughly, tugging the short black skirt from under her and lifting it over her hips. She pulled two chairs up to the table, positioned one on each side of her, and placed each of the maid's feet on one of them; then she pulled Natalie even further forward so that her buttocks were balanced on the very edge of the table. She took a knife, small and sharp, from the table, and pushed the maid's thighs even further apart. The knife disappeared between Natalie's legs, and Larry lunged forward with a sudden premonition of bloodshed; but Karen turned to him, holding out the dissected remains of Natalie's black nylon knickers.

'Smell them!' she said; and Larry breathed in Natalie's

most intimate perfumes. Karen turned back to the maid, once again keeping her gaze on Larry as her hands delved between Natalie's thighs, her crimson fingernails teasing the pubic curls, the fingers of her other hand sliding back and forth along the moistening slit, while the thumb rotated over the hidden button. Then Karen's hands returned to the maid's breasts, and remained there as the red-head lowered herself to bury her face in Natalie's gaping wet sex.

Larry could not see what Karen was doing with her mouth; and all he could hear were moist sucking noises and Natalie's occasional moans. He felt ready to explode.

At last Karen stood up. She licked her lips. Her fingers were holding open Natalie's labia, which appeared to be pulsating as if they had life of their own. 'Well, Larry,' she said, 'she's all yours.'

As if sleepwalking, Larry walked up to the maid and stepped into the space between her thighs. He placed his lips against hers, and she returned his kiss with a warm, damp enthusiasm that made his blood race in his veins. Karen stood behind him and encircled his body with her arms. He felt her breath against his shoulder and the points of her breasts hard against his back. Her fingers walked down his chest and stomach and began to unfasten his trousers. Almost afraid to look down at what Karen was doing, Larry kissed the maid with renewed fervour; and meanwhile Karen extracted his painfully erect member, caressing the stem with her palms as she directed the tip towards the opening between Natalie's thigh.

Larry gasped as his burning stiffness entered Natalie's cool softness. The moist, comfortable sheath seemed to relieve some of the pressures that had been building inside him. His body relaxed a little.

Karen pushed hard against his back, and he gasped again as his member thrust deeply into the maid and his hands made contact with her warm and spongy breasts. Karen pulled back, and then pushed again, pressing her chest into his back and grinding her hips against his backside; then she pulled back again, this time lowering Larry's trousers at the same time, leaving him naked from waist to ankles. The young man began to move rhythmically, backwards and forwards, diligently poking the maid's sex; and Karen whispered in his ear: 'Let's try something else, too.' Larry felt the red-head's hands massaging his buttocks, pulling them apart, and then a fingernail traced a line from the small of his back, along the furrow of his arse, and into his most intimate orifice. He jolted, as if he had suffered an electric shock, and almost spurted his sperm into Natalie. He had never been touched like that before. He felt violated. But, all the same, he bent forward and pushed his hips back, offering his rear to the red-head behind him.

Karen made him wait. While pushing her body against his to keep him firmly inside Natalie, who squeezed his penis and thrust her tongue into his mouth, Karen took a peach from one of the baskets. With her fingernails she peeled away the downy skin and then wrapped it around the second finger of her right hand. Thus equipped, she stabbed her finger deeply into the young man's back passage.

Larry sighed contentedly and murmured: 'No . . . Not that . . . '

Karen twisted her finger. Natalie placed her hands on Larry's hips and maintained his thrusts into her wet sex, but Larry found more pleasure now in the finger that was moving inside him, stretching his sphincter and widening the narrow opening as Karen's hand beat against his buttocks.

He started when Karen withdrew her finger, but the red-head merely told him to close his eyes. Natalie was watching his face and he felt he had no choice but to obey; but even as he lowered his eyes he saw Karen's hand taking a long, thin cucumber from the table. It had obviously been placed there for this very purpose. He felt the cool tip of the vegetable touch his puckered hole and moaned softly to himself. 'No . . . ' he said, making one last effort to protest; but Karen, with the cucumber held in front of her like a dildo, pushed into him gently but remorselessly. She no longer had to use any force: Larry's anus dilated and accepted the length and circumference of the cucumber. Larry almost fainted with a new and indescribable gratification.

Natalie caught Karen's eye and raised an eyebrow. Karen turned. Pierre, the butler, had silently entered the kitchen. He was wearing nothing but a tunic, which he opened to reveal his member, thick, erect, and purple. Karen stepped to one side, moved the cucumber back and forth a few times, and then removed it from Larry's anus. Before Larry had any idea what was happening, Pierre's aubergine replaced the cucumber. The butler siezed Larry's hips and penetrated him brutally with one stab; and Larry, suddenly aware of the hairy, muscular male body behind him, yelled with a mixture of pain, rage, and pleasure.

He tried to break free but Natalie held him, her arms around his neck, crushing his face into the soft mounds of her breasts. Behind him the butler withdrew a little, and then rammed into him again, and then again, plunging into the core of his body. Larry felt his flesh being bruised and stretched and torn, but at the same time he had never felt such enjoyment. Pierre's thrusts drove him ever more deeply into Natalie, who gave a little cry each time the combined weight of the two men bore into her; but just as Larry thought he was on the point of exploding within her, Pierre yanked him away.

Natalie slid along the table and jumped to the floor alongside Karen. The two young women embraced, kissed, and disappeared arm in arm.

Larry wanted to stop them, but he could not escape from

102

Pierre, who was pounding into his arse; and then he felt a burning jet flooding his insides as the butler reached his climax. Larry groaned with delight, and hardly felt Pierre withdrawing his penis. The butler lifted the young man, turned him round, and pressed his mouth against Larry's lips. Larry tried to flinch away, but feeling the strength of the butler's body against his, and the butler's hard, hot member against his stomach, he surendered to the kiss. He knew what was going to happen next.

Pierre's mouth slid from Larry's lips to his neck; across his chest; down his stomach; and closed round his throbbing prick. The butler advanced until Larry's penis touched the back of his throat; drew back, flicking his tongue along the stem; and then, as if suffering a convulsion, Larry arched his body, jerked spasmodically, and abandoned himself to an ecstasy that seemed to have no ending.

12

Nighttime, and silence. It seemed that the whole chateau was sleeping. Had it not been for the feeling that the small of his back had been lacerated and pummelled, Larry might have thought that he was dreaming — one of those erotic dreams in which nothing is too outrageous or too perverse. But he knew that he had not been dreaming. He had only to smell his hands to rediscover the mingled odours of Natalie and Pierre. They were two seriously weird servants, he reflected. And what about Karen? Where had she gone to? And how come she knew the house so well? Larry felt himself surrounded by a mystery so large that he was unable to see it. But this, he thought, was the least of his problems.

He had just learnt something about himself that was far more important. Not surprisingly, he had started to wonder about his sexual preferences some years before. He had been surprised at his own lack of enthusiasm for dating girls.

But in the end girls had proved to be no problem. He had simply copied his friends, and that had proved very successful. He did not share their excitement in the chase and in new conquests; each woman was the same to him — at first a chore, and then a bore. Now he was prepared to admit to himself that he had always been more excited after a baseball game, when the team was naked and strident and wet from the shower, than when he found himself in bed with even the prettiest of girls. In bed with a girl, he would do his duty; once his urge had been satisfied, he would start wanting to leave. He would become surly and restless. Once a girlfriend had experienced this treatment two or three times, she would lose any desire to see him again. This suited

Larry: he gained a reputation as the campus skirt-chaser.

Now Larry understood his feelings. Until this evening he had never experienced real pleasure. Pierre's body had mounted him, invaded him, humiliated him, and had thus revealed to him his true nature: So − I guess I'm a homosexual, he said to himself. He said it aloud, and his voice echoed strangely along the corridors of the dark chateau. 'Faggot!' he shouted, several times. 'Faggot! Bum boy!' And he added, in a murmur: 'James Pembroke, your son is gay.'

And that was the root of the problem. James Pembroke had publicly bankrolled several campaigns in support of traditional morality. AIDS, in his opinion, was God's punishment for sinners; the cities of America, he said, were governed by the ungodly and the impure, and he advocated cleaning them out by any means available. According to his simple principles, fags, dykes and commies were all part of the same insidious movement; and he believed that if you were one of those things, you were also more or less bound to be the others.

Larry's forehead broke out in a sweat when he thought about what would happen if his father found out. Then he snapped out of it: there was no question of relinquishing his new-found enjoyments merely for the sake of his father's public − and publicity-conscious − principles.

With this decision behind him, Larry relaxed. It remained to be seen whether he had the courage to stand up to his father's rages, threats and curses; but what the hell! he thought − time will tell. Meanwhile, he would continue his perambulation of the chateau and try to remember all the events and sensations of the evening.

He found himself in the main entrance hall. It was a warm night: he pulled open the doors and wandered outside. He saw a shadow − someone sitting on the steps of the staircase that led from the drive to the house. He recognised Jane's blonde hair. She was leaning against the stone balustrade, her skirt hitched up and her legs widely parted, and she was gazing up at the stars. She heard her brother approaching and without turning said: 'Hello, Larry.'

He put a hand on her shoulder and caressed her neck underneath her hair. She moved her head, gently, with the rhythm of his hand. 'What are you doing out here?' he asked.

Jane made no reply. Larry sat next to her. They stayed like that for a while, unmoving, breathing in the perfumes of the nearby forest — mosses, flowers, damp wood. At last Larry spoke. 'What a crazy night.'

He put an arm round his sister's shoulders and pulled her close. They cuddled against each other. 'It's a long time since we hugged each other,' Jane said.

'Tonight — tonight it seemed like a good idea.'

'It's almost as if we were very close to each other.'

Larry smiled. 'You mean, like brother and sister?'

'Brother and sister,' Jane said; and then remained quiet for a while, before saying, in a voice that was scarcely audible: 'It's strange, but — it feels like we're together the way we used to be.'

Larry blushed. Childhood memories rushed all too easily into his head. He remembered the June afternoon when his father had come upon them, naked, in Jane's bed, kissing each other's lips and caressing each other's bodies. In the midst of his towering rage James Pembroke had torn the sheet of the bed — and revealed his son's small but very obviously rigid penis. The children had been terrified, but, surprisingly, their father never mentioned the incident again. But their governess had been required to pack her bags that very same evening.

Larry felt that he needed to discuss the exact details of that scene; it reminded him of others in bathrooms, bedrooms, and showers. In particular, he remembered that as a child — in fact until only a few years ago — he had enjoyed accompanying his sister on shopping expeditions

106

because he was able to share the changing room with her when she was trying on a new brassiere or swimming costume. As he and his sister had become older, some of the sales assistants were shocked by this behaviour; but the Pembroke family were above suspicion − and not the kind of customers that any store would want to offend.

'I remember − ' Larry began.

'Hush,' said his sister, covering his mouth with her hand. 'I remember, too, but there's no point in talking about it.'

She sat up and looked straight into Larry's eyes. She hesitated, and then said: 'I have something to tell you. I guess maybe I should talk to Mom about this, but I just can't. She wouldn't understand, anyway. When you came out here and found me, that's when I knew you're the only one I can talk to.'

Larry kissed her lips, as if to stop her from going on. 'Don't say a thing,' he said. 'Whatever you've seen, whatever you've been through, those thing belong to nobody but you. There's no way you could begin to put all that into words. Between the two of us, brother and sister, sometimes there's no point in talk . . . '

'I guess you're right. Anyway, I don't know that I could find the right words . . . '

Larry had been speaking for himself as much as to his sister. He was still preoccupied by the episode in the kitchen and the discoveries he had made about himself. 'Words don't always explain everything,' he whispered.

He had never spoken to her in this way before. Perhaps she had had a flash of feminine intuition; perhaps her perceptions had been sharpened by the initiation she had just experienced; perhaps there was something in her brother's voice − something almost imperceptible − a more grown-up tone. She turned and looked at him for some time before saying: 'It seems to me you're not like you used to be. Has something serious happened to you?'

'It's that obvious?'

She had no time to reply that from now on nothing to do with sex would escape her notice; Larry motioned to her to keep silent. He pointed to a white limousine that was slowly approaching along the avenue. At first it was no more than a massive shape; then the sound of the engine could be heard as the vehicle advanced between the lines of trees.

'Who can that be?' Larry whispered.

'Search me,' Jane replied; but her heart was thumping in her chest. She hoped — and at the same time feared — that it was O, returning to find her again, to deliver her into the hands of more men, to make her submit to the whip, perhaps, or to the probings of fingers and tongues.

The car stopped at the edge of the lawn, as if the driver feared he would awaken the household if he came any closer. One of the doors opened and a woman emerged from the car.

'Holy shit!' Larry exclaimed.

It was Sally Pembroke who was standing next to the car, leaning into it to speak to the driver. Her voice carried to her children sitting on the steps. 'Goodnight, Karl, and thank you. I've had a wonderful evening.'

Sally smiled apologetically. 'No, that's not what I wanted to say,' she went on. 'That all sounds so polite and banal. You understand, don't you?'

Karl stepped out of the car. 'Of course,' he said with a brilliant smile, and offered his arm to her. Together they walked towards the steps leading up to the front doors of the chateau. Sally was so absorbed in her escort that she failed to notice her children, huddled closely together and amazed at the scene presented by their mother. Sally placed her hand round Karl's. It was slender hand, she thought, elegant and yet strong. She sighed.

'I'm really happy that O introduced us to each other,' she said. 'But there I go again, talking in clichés. I guess I just can't talk naturally any more.'

108

Karl stopped. 'You succeeded in doing so all evening,' he said.

'Well then, it must be this place. It does something to me. We colonials can't help being impressed by a pile of old stones.' She laughed and held the young man's hand more tightly. 'But don't you believe it. More polite nothings. The truth is — I don't know how to say goodbye to you.'

They had reached the first steps of the staircase. Karl took Sally's other hand, drew her to him, and kissed her gently on the lips. 'Like this, my dear Sally,' he murmured.

A light was switched on in the hall. James Pembroke, looking almost imperial in a scarlet dressing-gown, appeared in the doorway, a pocket calculator in his hand. 'Is it too much to ask to be allowed to work in peace?' he grumbled.

'I'm sorry, honey,' Sally said, climbing a few steps towards him. 'I didn't know you were still working.' She turned towards Karl. 'This young man was kind enough to bring me home from the party.'

James shrugged, gave Karl a contemptuous glance, and muttered: 'Thanks, buddy. Don't forget to turn off the lights when you're through. And don't talk too loud — it disturbs me when I'm working.'

He was turning to go when he caught sight of Larry and Jane, who had not moved from the steps. 'What are you two doing there, sitting in the dark?'

Brother and sister had no time to reply. Natalie and Pierre appeared in the hall, fully dressed in their servants' uniforms as if they had not undressed since the Pembroke family had arrived at the chateau. Pierre went up to James. 'We heard a noise,' he said. 'Do you need anything, Monsieur Pembroke?'

'Hell, no. Everything's fine.' He examined Natalie's face, and then Pierre's. They remained expressionless. James was irritated; he felt that something was going on, something that eluded him. 'Always ready, aren't you? Don't you take those monkey suits off even when you go to bed?'

The maid stepped forward, leant towards him, and said: 'Whatever you wish, *monsieur*.'

His eyes drawn to Natalie's plunging neck-line, James felt a stirring of lust; but this was no time for daydreams, he told himself, and certainly not for daydreams about a servant girl. 'Good night, everybody,' he said firmly, and then, turning to Sally, added: 'Take as long as you want with this young fellow; but make sure you come by my room when you're through with him — me and you have things to do together.' And he laughed harshly as he strode into the hall.

'James! How dare you!' Sally snarled; she turned to Karl and said: 'I'm really sorry about this.'

Larry and Jane stood up, blew kisses to their mother, and said goodnight. Sally waved distractedly in their direction, and they decided not to wait for any further acknowledgement. As they passed Pierre and Natalie, Larry feigned indifference; and the servants betrayed no hint of their complicity in the evening's events, standing straight and still and suggesting the deference and readiness to serve that is common to all good domestic staff. Larry, however, was beset with memories stirred up by the sight of Pierre and Natalie: the hot, humid sex of the maid, and — even more exciting — the butler's rigid and powerful member.

The servants waited silently until Larry and Jane were on their way to their rooms; and then, without a word, they withdrew into the house.

Karl and Sally were alone. He offered her a Turkish cigarette; she hesitated, and then took one in the hope that he would not leave while they were smoking together. At that moment she wanted nothing more than to keep Karl with her a little longer. 'I wonder,' she said, 'how long the kids were sitting there . . . '

'Surely it cannot matter,' Karl replied.

'Not to you, maybe. I'm their mother, remember?'

'Let me assure you that tonight they have other things on their minds.'

Sally stared at him. 'What do you know about it? You don't even know these kids.'

'I know,' Karl said decisively.

Sally kept silent. She was thinking how oddly everything was working out: O, with her emerald-green gaze; the confidences that Sally had willingly volunteered; and this young man, almost too handsome, too elegant, and so very sure of himself . . . She shivered. Karl raised a questioning eyebrow.

'I was thinking about my husband,' she explained. 'I feel so ashamed.'

'But why?'

'Oh, he's so . . . '

'Brutal? Even brutality can have a certain charm.'

'Are you always like this? Always such a smart-ass?' Sally demanded; and when he didn't reply, she added: 'And are you always this cool?'

'There is nothing to be uncool about,' Karl said. 'We are doing nothing wrong.'

Not yet, Sally thought; but out loud she said: 'Of course not. You and I know that. But I can guess what the children might have been thinking, sitting there in the dark, listening to me carrying on like a schoolgirl.'

Karl seemed bored. 'There is no reason for you to feel guilty. Or even to think that you made yourself look ridiculous.'

It was a deliberately insolent reply. Sally straightened. She allowed her husband to treat her inconsiderately, but she did not grant the same liberty to anyone else – not even this seductive young man. She was Mrs James Pembroke, one of the premier ladies in the USA, conscious of her wealth and position. 'I do not feel guilty,' she said in a dry voice.

Karl did not react. 'I have nothing to feel guilty about,'

111

she went on. 'And I never shall.' And she took Karl's face between her hands and pulled his lips to her mouth, her tongue searching for his. Then, as suddenly, she pushed him away.

'That's enough!' she said.

Karl showed no surprise. 'You are mixed up,' he said. 'You kiss me, you send me away — '

'I told you,' Sally said. 'I don't want to feel guilty. Let's just say it's my safety-net.'

Karl threw his cigarette on to the lawn. 'You are quite simply wrong,' he sneered. 'A little guilt adds spice.'

'Don't try to be cynical. You'll never be able to beat James at that.'

'I have absolutely no intention of entering into a competition with your husband,' Karl said calmly; and when Sally merely shrugged her shoulders he took her by the wrists and pulled her towards him. 'I'm no cynic. I just know what I like.'

'And that is?'

'This,' he said, and buried his face in her hair and then covered her naked shoulders with kisses.

At first Sally made no protest, but at last she tried to pull away. 'I already kissed you goodbye, Karl. Now stop it. Stop it, Karl!'

'OK. I can stop. But you don't really want me to.'

Sally took a step backward. Karl remained unmoved. 'I was told you were looking for a gigolo,' he said.

'How dare you!' Sally's anger flared, and then subsided under the realisation that Karl's insolence excited her as much as her husband's callousness.

The young man stepped close to her again. 'I am not a gigolo,' he said. 'If I were, I would not tell you the truth like this. I would be too worried about annoying you. But I find it amusing to play the part of a gigolo. And you like it, too. You are quite ready to move on to the actions that

112

our roles suggest; it is only the words that frighten you.'

Sally wanted to hurt him. 'That's one hell of a flimsy philosophy,' she said, putting into her voice as much scorn as she could muster. He curled an arm round her waist and pulled her towards him. She struggled vainly against his muscular arms, and yielded at last, saying: 'Oh well. At least actions can't lie.'

Karl caressed her shoulders, and stroked the back of her neck. Sally could no longer deny the desire that she felt growing inside her; but she remained angry because she was sure that the young man, too, was aware of her desire. She was angry with his smooth, self-confident voice. 'It is true that to begin with,' he said, 'I came along for just a bit of fun. But now, Sally — now I like you. I like you very much.'

'Of all the corny..! Do you expect me to believe that?'

He pulled her body against his. She felt the stiff pole of his sex against her stomach. 'Of course,' he said. 'Because it's true.'

'Do you think I'm some kind of idiot?'

'All I know is that I want you.'

'Is that so? You're one mule-headed kid. But you'll never convince me.'

'Well — perhaps not.'

Sally placed her hand against Karl's rigid member. He remained still. 'This is more like it,' she said. 'I prefer you as a gigolo. It suits your personality.'

Karl bowed, and brushed his lips down Sally's neck from earlobe to shoulder. 'I shall be whatever you desire,' he said.

'OK. So let's go,' Sally declared.

'Where?'

'Wherever you want. It's no big deal. Your place?'

'In the car,' Karl said.

'That's just perfect,' Sally sighed, resting her head against his chest. 'I've been fucking in comfort for the last twenty years. You're no competition for James in that area, either.'

113

13

Sally Pembroke herself would find it difficult to give a coherent account of what happened next.

Karl escorted her to the white limousine parked at the edge of the lawn. Sally draped herself across the fawn leather of the back seat; she let her head fall back and shuddered with anticipation. She opened her legs almost unconsciously, leaving one foot on the floor and lifting the other on to the seat. Karl got into the car beside her, wedging her leg between his ribcage and the back of the seat as he sat between her thighs. His hands pulled at her dress, revealing the expanses of bare flesh above the tops of her stockings. His fingers caressed the pale skin, and strayed more and more persistently across the pink silk of her knickers, at first merely brushing against the warm soft centre between the tops of her legs, and then pushing insistently against the damp silk.

He stopped for a moment to listen to Sally's hoarse and rapid pants of breath; and then he seized the knickers in his hands and tore them apart, yanking the shreds of cloth from her body. He gazed at thick bush of golden curls he had revealed; then he placed his fist below it and pushed hard into her intimate parts. Sally shivered, and parted her thighs even more widely, and lifted her body towards his hard and intrusive hand.

'Fuck me! Come on, fuck me!' she cried out as Karl was unbuttoning his trousers, releasing his prick and pointing it at her impatient hole.

Karl lay across her, covering her with the weight of his body, his member probing gently but not penetrating her.

She locked her arms round him and pulled him into her. He started to move slowly, backwards and forwards, inducing little cries of pleasure from Sally, who found that the discomfort of her position somehow added to her enjoyment. Suddenly angry, she raked her nails across his backside, and then pushed him away.

'Karl,' she said in a low voice, 'I'm sure you're a real expert lover. But when a woman like me decides to two-time a husband like mine, she expects a bit less in the way of consideration. You can do better than this.'

He ceased his movements. 'Better?'

'Sure. What's the point of playing the field if all I get is what James gives me every day?'

'I see. Very well, let us see if you can take it. From now on, you are simply a sexual object. Just a tart, for me to enjoy. Get up!'

'What?' Sally tried to move, but was crushed beneath the young man's body. She tried to push him off her, but he seized her hands and dragged her out of the car.

'Come on, whore! Get out!'

He pushed her against the side of the white limousine. She tried to run, but found that her legs would not support her. Karl grabbed her arm, turned her towards him, and slapped her face so hard that tears of shock and rage sprang from her eyes. 'Now,' he said through gritted teeth, 'now you're going to do what I tell you.'

Sally made a last attempt to struggle, but it was useless. Karl was stronger than she, and more determined. She looked towards the chateau, but realised that there was no hope of expecting any help. Only one window, that of her husband's room, remained lit. Even if she shouted, he would not be able to hear her. She realised now why the young man had stopped the car so far from the house. She had fallen into a trap, and she would have to submit to everything that Karl demanded of her. Nothing – not her pleas, nor her orders, nor even her money — could stop the young man now.

Sally was surprised to find that her fear had in no way diminished her lust. In her heart she welcomed the sudden violence, the unpredictability. More than ever before, she craved satisfaction. She wanted Karl's body, and his huge prick, and his considered brutality.

The young man was cool and deliberate, his actions precise: a well-rehearsed actor who knew exactly what to do. His strong hands forced her against the car, grasped the bodice of her dress, and tore it in half. Sally, the wife of a multi-millionaire, was naked and helpless at the hands of a stranger in a foreign country. The fact that she was still wearing a suspender belt and stockings only increased her feeling of complete nudity. She shivered, and tried to cover her breasts with her hands. Karl slapped her face again, pushed down her arms, and delivered an agonising slap to each of her tits.

He waited until she was still, and facing him again. He took both her thick, hard nipples between his fingers and thumbs, and watched her face. He pulled; he twisted and squeezed. Sally opened her mouth in pain, but kept her hands againt the metal of the car and leant towards the young man, as if offering him more of herself. With a sneer he released her, and pushed her towards the front of the vehicle.

Sally stood between the car's headlights. Her dark-blonde hair, dishevelled and windswept, flew from side to side as she scanned the darkness. Karl watched her impassively. He extended a foot, and nudged her legs apart; and then he stepped forward to place a hand between her thighs. He pushed two fingers inside her, and grinned; Sally was consumed, simultaneously, with shame and pleasure.

With sharp thrusts of his other hand, Karl pushed her against the car's radiator, which was warm against the backs

116

of her thighs. He kept on pushing, and Sally found herself leaning backwards, eventually lying on her back on the bonnet of the car. Karl's fingers were still inside her, but now, abruptly, he withdrew. Sally moaned, and tried to slide off the car, but Karl took her by the hips and shoved her further on to the flat expanse of steel so that her head was almost touching the windscreen. Sally stared up at the stars in the night sky, aware that her legs were still dangling at the front of the car, and then that Karl had grasped her left ankle. It took a few moments for her to realise that he had tied a rope around the ankle and was securing it to one end of the car's front bumper. She sat up, but Karl very calmly punched her in the stomach, and she collapsed, winded. Karl then proceeded to tie her other ankle to the other end of the bumper: her legs were stretched apart, and her gaping sex surmounted the radiator grille like a mascot. He looked down at her and smiled unpleasantly before tying her wrists to the mirrors on the car's front doors.

Sally could not move. She was tied to the car like a deer recently killed by hunters and being brought home in triumph. Her arms extended, her thighs spread apart, she was a sacrifice, offered to the gods of the night on a metal altar of wealth.

Sally could hear Karl moving round the car. She felt her arm being moved as a door opened and closed. Karl had re-entered the car, and was behind the steering wheel. He turned the ignition key, and Sally was aware of nothing but a throbbing vibration and the roar of the engine as Karl put his foot on the throttle. The car moved; Sally found that she was too terrified even to cry.

Karl drove the car slowly along the avenue of trees and into the forest; but to Sally it seemed that she was being propelled at breakneck speed. The wind lifted her hair and spread it like a fan across the windscreen; she was cold, she was surrounded by trees, she was deafened by the noise of

117

the engine, she was jolted by each bump in the woodland track. She sobbed and writhed silently, her face distorted by fear, pain racking her limbs.

The car stopped in a clearing. Even if she had tried, Sally would have had no way of getting her bearings; in fact she was now very close to the lodge in which O was staying. She suffered one more moment of intense pain as Karl brought the car to a halt and the ropes cut into her wrists.

Sally was dimly aware that Karl was leaving the car; but she did not see the slender form that emerged from the undergrowth to take his place behind the wheel. Even Karl could distinguish nothing of the figure but the green eyes that stared at him, ordering him to continue with the ceremony.

Karl went to the back of the car and returned with a whip. It was not large or heavy, but it had several braided leather lashes, each terminating in a hardened point. He stood alongside the bonnet of the car and held up the whip, waiting patiently until Sally turned her head towards him and focused her eyes on the instrument he was dangling above her face. Then he took one small step back, and proceeded to flog her.

He placed three brisk strokes across her stomach. Sally shrieked and arched her back, groaning as three bright lines appeared on her white flesh. Karl leant forward to inspect the effects of his handiwork; then, apparently satisfied with the results, he started to whip the pale and widely-separated hemispheres of her breasts.

His precise, evenly-weighted strokes alternated between the two mounds of flesh. First the splayed strands of leather would fall across Sally's right breast; then, when Sally had stopped squirming, Karl would take a half step backward and her left breast would receive the flailing tongues. Karl was meticulous: each stroke was hard enough to ensure that every lash left its mark, a thin red line ending in an even more firey point; but not so hard as to break the skin.

At last he stopped. Sally writhed in her bonds, and felt rivulets of sweat trickling across her belly and shoulders. Karl walked to the other side of the bonnet, positioned himself, and raised the whip again. Sally screamed in protest as the flogging was resumed. Only when the lattice of fine lines had merged to make both breasts a deep and angry pink; only when both lacerated nipples were standing erect and flaming like beacons did Karl cease whipping.

Each gust of cool night air was both a torture and a relief to Sally's bosom. She closed her eyes and drew in lungfuls of breath, unaware that Karl, whip in hand, was now standing between her outstretched legs. The first indication that her torment was not over was the hissing in the air as Karl swished the lashes upwards to land at the junction of her thighs, the tips cutting into her cunt and the tenderest flesh of her buttocks. He struck again, downwards, across the golden triangle of curling hair. And again, upwards. And again. And again.

Sally could only toss her head and sob as each stroke fell; and, as if providing a derisive commentary, the figure in the driving seat revved the car's engine in time with the falling of the whip. Nothing existed for Sally but the burning sensation between her legs; the heat of the bonnet under her buttocks and shoulders; the snarling vibration of the engine; and glimpses of Karl's emotionless face as he whipped her with methodical precision.

Finally, when Sally was beyond further humiliation and ceased all sound and movement apart from continuous sobs, the figure with the green eyes made a sign to Karl to stop.

The young man dropped the whip and undid his trousers. He placed his hands on Sally's hips and entered her with one sudden thrust. She let out a wail of surprise. Karl immediately withdrew, lifted and pulled apart her buttocks, and penetrated her rear. As he had promised, Sally was now nothing but an object, the instrument of his lust.

And each time that he entered her and left her, alternating between her front and rear passages, she felt a surge of mounting pleasure. It was inexorable, and she hated it. She wanted nothing more than to be able to push him away from her — except perhaps to clutch him to her, to hold his body, to embrace him. But her shackles prevented her from doing either.

She could not help reacting to Karl's insistent movements. With each thrust his member plunged deeply into her, and his body slammed against the sore and striated skin of her thighs and buttocks. With each thrust she felt her body shudder with pre-orgasmic tension; and each spasm was more powerful than the last.

She could sense that Karl, too, was approaching a climax. Without respite his member dug into her with insolent and mighty lunges. He did not look at her; to him, she was no more than an object. And this was part of her enjoyment, too; she revelled in his contempt for her reactions as he concentrated on fulfilling his own desires.

He stopped; and then pushed into her anus as deeply as he could, climbing on to the car's bumper in order to drive home his throbbing tool. He stayed there, unmoving, staring down at her expressionlessly; and Sally, impaled, discovered that there are violations within violations as she struggled to avoid his gaze.

Slowly and with unexpected care he withdrew his member from her, and advanced on hands and knees across the bonnet, straddling her torso. He placed his huge red rod between her breasts, and his hands on the burning mounds. Sally gasped at the touch, and moaned as he pressed against the raw flesh, moulding her tits around his hot organ.

She lifted her head, guessing that his climax was imminent. As she saw the first spurt of viscous fluid shoot from his tool and felt it splash on to her neck and chin, Karl dug his fingertips into her blazing tortured tits; and Sally screamed, abandoning herself to the pain and to an orgasm such as she had never imagined possible.

Karl grabbed her hair, and silenced her moans by stuffing his sex into her mouth. He told her to lick it. She obeyed. The taste of her own juices mingled with his caused her further ecstatic tremblings, and she was surprised to realise that she felt disappointed when he pulled away.

Calmly, with the indifference of a professional at work, Karl untied the ropes that secured her to the car. Sally, her mind and body still overwhelmed with ecstasy, slid from the bonnet and stood against the car. She turned, and at last saw the green eyes that were staring at her; and faster than thought she was submerged beneath yet another wave, an orgasmic tide that rippled upwards from her arse to her entrails.

14

Daniel Botterweg drove slowly along the Bois de Boulogne. He was steering with one hand, as he was also enjoying himself watching the prostitutes, half-naked in their cars, as they attracted their clients. It was still early in the afternoon, but there were plenty of punters. As soon as one of the girls enticed a man into her car, a crowd of voyeurs would surge after them in the hope of catching a glimpse of their furtive acts in the thick of the woods.

A discreet buzzer sounded inside the metallic-grey Mercedes. Botterweg had been expecting the call. He picked up the telephone and recognised the voice of James Pembroke: 'Botterweg?'

'Yes, Monsieur Pembroke. You are very punctual.'

'I hate to waste time. I hope that goes for you too.'

Botterweg smiled to his reflection in the rear view mirror. 'Don't worry, Pembroke. You won't be wasting your precious time.'

'I better not be,' growled the American.

'Where are you?' Botterweg asked.

There was a brief silence. Botterweg imagined Pembroke sitting in the back of his black limousine and leaning forward to consult his chauffeur. Then Pembroke's voice said: 'Avenue de la Grande-Armee.'

'Excellent. I'm waiting for you in the woods, by the *Grand Lac*.'

'This whole set-up is kids' stuff. I'm not getting into some boy scout orienteering exercise.'

'It's in your interests that I'm taking these precautions, Monsieur Pembroke.'

'My interests? Hell, we could fix up the whole thing on the phone.'

'Please have a little patience. You will soon be there — and I assure you, you will not regret it.'

Botterweg replaced the receiver. He was about to play a difficult hand against a wily opponent. He needed to think before the confrontation.

Before long he saw, in his wing mirror, the black limousine gliding along the edge of the lake. He waited until the car had passed in front of his Mercedes; he wanted to be sure that Pembroke was unaccompanied, although he was fairly sure that this was an unnecessary precaution. The multi-millionaire was not the kind of man to think that he needed help or protection; he was sure he could stand up to anyone, and certainly to this little fellow Botterweg about whom he knew little except that he was Henri Carel's right-hand man.

Botterweg flashed his headlights. The limousine drew in to the side of the road, and Botterweg slid his car alongside the pavement and parked behind it. He got out; Pembroke joined him, ignoring the hand that Botterweg extended in greeting.

'Well? What do you want?' James barked.

Botterweg indicated a path that meandered next to the lake. 'Shall we take a little stroll?'

'Come on, Botterweg. Put your cards on the table. I'm not here to tiptoe through the tulips with you.'

Botterweg made no reply; instead, he set off along the path. James cursed under his breath and set off in pursuit.

'Lovely day, isn't it?' Botterweg said when the American had caught up with him.

'You've got one minute. And not a second more.'

Botterweg sighed. 'All this haste . . . It's why you Americans fail in some of your dealings, you know. You seem to be unable to adapt to European ways. Here we

123

require a certain decorum. Civilisation, Pembroke, manners – these are the distinguishing marks of human beings.'

These remarks reminded James of his wife's comments on the evening that they had arrived in France. You'd think they'd talked it over beforehand! Well, they were wasting their breath. His laugh echoed across the lake. 'Little man,' he said, 'I have never once screwed up a deal. Not in the USA; not in little old Europe. Not even in Africa.'

'I know that. You are very tough. That's why you don't fool me.' He stopped in the middle of the path and turned to face Pembroke. 'You have no intention of acquiring Capitol Industries.'

James gave a sarcastic whistle. 'Well is that so? And how in hell can you be sure of that?'

'It's the way you are handling the affair, Pembroke. You have been in France for several days now. You would usually settle matters more quickly than this.'

'Let's just say I'm taking the opportunity to enjoy a break – a family holiday.'

Botterweg shook his head. 'We'll see about that . . . But in any case, I possess certain interesting pieces of information.'

'Like what?'

'All cards on the table?'

'Don't be naive, Botterweg. You know how to play poker – you don't show until the end of the game. After all the stakes are on the table and it's too late to back out.'

'As you wish. I'll raise the bidding. You do intend to buy us, Pembroke – but only in order to sell us again, for a profit. In other words, you're only in this as a broker – a middleman.'

'That's some imagination you've got.'

'I don't need testimonials from you.'

'In any case, as far as you're concerned, the bottom line's the same: you get bought.'

124

'Not entirely the same, Pembroke. I would like you to guarantee me first refusal when you dispose of Capitol.'

James bent down and picked up a pebble. He skimmed it across the still water of the lake. It bounced three times. 'When I was a boy, I could do seven,' he said with a rueful smile. 'Guess I've lost the knack.'

Botterweg grabbed a stone and threw it towards the lake. It sank with a loud plop.

'Botterweg,' James laughed, 'you are just not the right size for this kind of game.'

Without replying, Botterweg selected another pebble, flat and almost rectangular. He concentrated, studied the lake, and hurled the missile. It hit the water and bounced five more times before disappearing.

'Not bad,' James conceded. 'But just kids' stuff. Business isn't child's play. You think I'm going to give you this first option as a birthday present, maybe?'

'Of course not, Pembroke. First of all, this deal will benefit you. I have the backing of three banks − please don't expect me to name them. I want Carel's job. We are offering one hundred and twenty dollars a share, which is considerably more than you will have to pay out.'

'Sure, it's a tempting offer. But I want to keep Capitol Industries for myself.'

'And I thought you weren't interested in wasting time!' Botterweg said sarcastically. A swan floated by, its head erect, its plumage smooth and white. Casually, Botterweg added: 'And as I mentioned, I have certain information.'

'Maybe so,' James said. 'But what's to stop Henri Carel making me a better offer than yours?'

'I have nothing to fear from Carel.'

'What does that mean?'

'I don't think you will want to do business with him.'

'Explain yourself, damn you!'

Botterweg appeared to be embarassed. 'I would rather not.'

'You're very cautious, all of a sudden.'

'I will have to tell you things that you will not find particularly agreeable . . . '

'I'll be the judge of that!'

James forced himself to remain calm. He had enough experience of negotiations to know that this time his adversary was not bluffing. He had a winning card and he was going to play it. But shrewd as he was, James was not expecting what he heard.

'You have been tricked,' Botterweg said. 'The house in which you are staying has been set up to get you and your family involved in an enormous sex scandal.'

'This is some kind of a joke?'

'Not at all. I told you that you wouldn't like it.'

'My family is above suspicion.'

'But not beyond temptation.' Botterweg kept his eyes on his shoes, which he was shuffling like a naughty schoolboy in the headmaster's study. He spoke in a whisper, even though they were alone on the lakeside path. 'There are videos, photographs, tape recordings . . . Your wife, your daughter, your son . . . all compromised. If even one piece of this evidence were to be published, your reputation would be ruined.'

James furrowed his brow. 'Carel's your boss,' he said calmly. 'What's to stop him using them?'

'I've made sure that he'll do nothing.'

'How?'

Botterweg smiled. He felt absolutely sure of himself now. The American's questions merely revealed the extent to which he had resigned himself to the situation. Botterweg – Chairman and Managing Director of Capitol Industries! He had been dreaming of it for years, and now he it was about to happen. 'I have documents,' he explained, 'which prove that the whole plot against you was Carel's idea, and carried out on his instructions. If he tries to make use of any of the material, he will be compromised too.'

'You bastard!' James muttered.

'Pardon?' asked Botterweg, who had heard perfectly.

'Nothing,' James said, reproaching himself for losing his self-control. He tried to breathe deeply, as his cardiologist advised every month. 'But even if I agree to this scam of yours, Botterweg, Carel can still put in an offer when I put Capitol up for sale.'

Botterweg shook his head. 'By then it will be too late,' he said. 'The deal between you and my partners will already be finalised.'

James gave an appreciative whistle. 'Well played, Botterweg.'

The little man bowed. 'I have been an admirer of yours for some time, Monsieur Pembroke. I have studied your methods. An excellent education.'

James put his hand on Botterweg's shoulder. The little man flinched. With sharp, hard shoves James pushed him towards the lake. Botterweg tried to escape but James herded him remorselessly to the edge of the water, stopping only when the heels of Botterweg's shoes were being lapped by the ripples.

'Just the same,' James gritted, 'there's a hole in your scheme, Botterweg. How are you going to deal with my reaction? My personal reaction?'

Botterweg sidled away. From a little distance, and feeling more secure, he said: 'I am sure you are above all a businessman, Monsieur Pembroke. You will decide on the profitable course of action.' He stepped back on to the path and smiled. 'And are we not all gentlemen?'

'You should consult a dictionary, Botterweg. Some of the definitions of the word "gentleman" will come as quite a shock.'

Botterweg waited for the American to join him on the

path. 'Let us not stray into futile arguments about semantics, Pembroke. Can I assume that we have a deal?'

James stepped past him; he hurried to catch up.

'Let me have this evidence you claim to have.'

'All the material is nearby,' Botterweg said. 'It's safely away from prying eyes. I'll give it all to you as soon as you've signed the papers at my bankers'. Do we have a deal?'

'I wouldn't call it a deal. It gives me no pleasure to accept your offer. Don't think this makes us pals, Botterweg. I don't take kindly to blackmail.'

'That expression is equally repugnant to me, I assure you. I know I am taking some risks. I would prefer it if we could talk about business rather than blackmail.'

'Now who's straying into futile semantic arguments? Eh, Botterweg?'

The little man gave him a honeyed smile. He had won the first round, and was happy to let James Pembroke humiliate him now. It was a small price to pay for the Chairmanship of Capitol Industries.

Botterweg had had copies of some of the photographs in his Mercedes. One look had been enough for James. He knew what was going on; he had burnt the prints. As he watched the bodies and faces of his family being engulfed by the flames, he promised himself that he would deal with them later. In the meantime, he had to act; to combat this little fellow Botterweg who had the nerve to tell him what to do.

In the back of his limousine, he was tapping on the keyboard of his computer. URGENT. FULL REPORT: DANIEL BOTTERWEG. FULL REPORT: O (WOMAN, OWNER OF HOUSE USED FOR STAY IN FRANCE.)

The message SEARCH IN PROGRESS appeared on the screen in green letters. James broke the modem connection

128

and dialled a New York number. 'Ginsberg? Pembroke. Where are we on the Capitol acquisition?'

Ginsberg's nasal voice answered. 'As at nine this morning we can secure one and a half million shares.'

'OK, fine. We have to sew it up real fast. Last night's Wall Street price?'

'Eighty dollars.'

'I can resell at a hundred and twenty.'

There was a respectful silence at the other end of the line. 'Forty dollars a share!' Ginsberg yelled at last. 'Sixty million dollars instant profit!'

'You don't say. I can do the multiplication myself, thanks.'

James hung up. He frowned: he still had to do the most difficult part. He picked up the telephone again and called the chateau. Pierre answered. James paused; all these French sounded the same to him, and after Botterweg's revelations he didn't know who he could expect to find at the house. He had to be sure.

'Is that you, Pierre?'

'Of course, monsieur.'

'Good. I want to see O. Immediately. Do you know where I can find her?'

'Yes, monsieur. The mistress is using the small summer house.'

'OK, but where?'

'At the far end of the estate, monsieur.'

'Are you telling me that she's living just a couple of hundred yards from us?'

'Certainly, monsieur.'

The butler's diplomacy was beginning to annoy him. He restrained himself from making a few well-chosen remarks; this was not the time to risk losing face. All these folk are in it together, he reminded himself; they all want to see me brought down. Well, they're not going to get that pleasure.

129

He forced his voice into a polite and peaceful tone, as if he were asking for directions to a restaurant. 'And how do I get there?'

'Turn to the left, after you come in through the gate. The track follows the wall that surrounds the estate. Jean knows the way.'

'Who's this guy Jean?'

'Your chauffeur, monsieur.'

'Him too, huh?'

'He also what, monsieur?'

James didn't bother to answer that. Instead he said: 'Tell O I'll be there right away.'

He hung up. For the first time since his adolescence he had sweaty hands.

15

The chauffeur drove through the gate and turned immediately into a lane that was so well concealed by trees that it was hardly noticeable. The car swished through the forest for some time, and James was surprised at the vast extent of O's estate. Once again he found himself wondering about this strange and evidently wealthy woman.

In a clearing in the depths of the woods the black limousine halted at last outside a hunting lodge.

'This is the place?' Pembroke asked; the chauffeur nodded. James never felt nervous when confronting an adversary, but he was nervous now. He shook his head, cleared his throat, and lit a Davidoff before climbing the few steps to the front door.

As he was reaching for the brass knocker, the door opened. A young woman stood in the doorway. James was taken aback by her bizarre appearance, but he had to admit that she was attractive. As on the previous evening, when she had opened the door to Jane, she was wearing a full-skirted dress with a bodice that pushed forward her half-exposed bosom; her eyes were black with kohl and her lipstick was purple. She stood aside to allow James to enter, and said: 'Madame is expecting you.'

She led him to a large room with windows that overlooked the parkland of the estate. James noticed a stable-block jutting at a right angle from the lodge.

O was sitting on cushions on the floor. She was wearing an opal-blue tunic of shantung silk that was so light that it was almost transparent. She was barefoot; and she radiated a sense of youthful innocence. James could hardly

131

believe that this was the same person, the horsewoman and chess-player, who had called on him on his first morning in the chateau.

But he was not going to allow himself to be distracted by what he saw as a deliberately staged scene. He marched up to O, stood in front of her, and demanded: 'Who are you working for?'

O gave him a long, clear, emerald-green look. Her body, unrestricted and almost naked, seemed like a reflection of the dazzling summer light. 'Why don't you sit down?' she said.

James clenched his fists. This woman had a knack for annoying him. 'Who are you working for?' he repeated.

'Whatever you want,' she said; and rose to her feet with a supple, graceful movement that widened the opening of her tunic. James glimpsed the brown tip of a breast, and felt his throat tighten. O went to the windows and stretched in the sunlight. 'You know,' she said, without turning to face him, 'you're by no means the first person to ask that question. I'll give the answer that I always give.' She came up to him and took his arm. 'I don't work for anyone. In fact, I don't work at all.'

James felt like slapping her. Instead, he yelled at her. 'You can do better than that. I want some answers and I'll get them, one way or another.'

O made no move except to lean slightly towards him. 'Are you threatening me, James?' she said, almost conspiratorily.

He grabbed her wrists and pulled her against him. 'Yes,' he said roughly, 'I'm sure as hell threatening you.'

O freed herself from his grasp. 'And to what do I owe this honour?'

'Quit fooling, O. I'm not about to waste any more time. I know!'

'You know what?'

James refused to be taken in by the young woman's apparent surprise. He had reached his decision. To hell with civilised behaviour! If he had to, he'd beat her until she was ready to talk. In fact, deep down, he found himself looking forward to the prospect; but for the moment he forced himself to remain calm. 'Daniel Botterweg has told me everything. Everything, you understand? My wife, my son, my daughter . . . And Carel's plot . . . '

O took the news with every appearance of tranquility, as if he had been describing a film he had just seen. 'I suppose he has his reasons for doing so,' was all she said.

James was determined to appear equally unconcerned. He relit his cigar. 'That lighter makes the room stink of petrol!' O said, taking a box of matches from a low table. 'Use these next time.'

Without thinking, he pocketed the box of matches. 'Botterweg has his reasons,' he said, 'and I know what they are. Right now it's your reasons that interest me.'

He drew on his cigar, and at that moment Bruno ran into the room, his mouth hanging open and his tongue lolling. Ignoring his master, he stretched out beside O. 'Bruno!' James shouted in surprise. 'What in hell is that dog doing here?'

O leant to scratch Bruno's head, and the dog gave a yelp of pleasure. 'He hasn't left the lodge for several days,' she said. 'Perhaps he prefers the food here.'

James felt the same sensation of disquiet that he sometimes felt during a game of chess, at the moment of losing a major piece and realising that his king was threatened. Bruno's defection to O's side seemed like an omen of defeat. 'I get the picture,' he said. 'Seems nobody can resist you. Not even dogs.'

O took his arm and led him to the windows, where they were bathed in sunlight. The dog followed them, his nose pressed against O's legs. 'James,' she said gently, 'you are

133

asking such childish questions. Questions that don't deserve to be answered.'

James growled with fury. O quietened him with a smile. 'But if you like,' she said, 'I'll tell you what you're doing here.'

'I know what I'm doing here!'

'I'm not so sure. For instance, you claim to be defending your family. But you must know that you have no reason to worry. If Botterweg has revealed to you what he knows, and has done a deal with you, then obviously he and his friends will have no interest in raising a scandal. As for me: anything that I know will remain a secret. You have always known that, really.'

She fixed her green gaze on James, who made sure that his expression neither confirmed or denied what she was saying. 'The thing that is worrying you,' she went on, 'is this: who is behind Botterweg?'

'Do you know?' he said, perhaps too eagerly.

'Oh, James!' O sighed reproachfully.

'Tell me!' he demanded.

'Are you sure? It's not as if you don't already know what I'm going to say to you.'

James scowled at her. 'Well,' she went on, 'we now come to the heart of the matter, Monsieur James Pembroke. Which is me; O. O attracts you; O fascinates you. Not just as a woman; but because she can get what she wants.'

This was too much for James. He took a vicarious revenge by kicking Bruno in the groin. The dog yelped in pain and, whining, ran to take shelter behind a sofa. O shook her head. 'That works with dogs,' she said, 'but not with me.'

James noticed that O's riding-crop was lying on the table. It was a small one, made of black leather. He picked it up and went back to O. 'We shall see,' he said. 'You're too sure of yourself, O. You don't know me very well yet.'

'If this will give you pleasure,' she sighed, and let her tunic slip to the floor. Naked, she turned away from James and knelt on the floor, offering him her back. 'Carry on,' she said, lowering her head and lifting her buttocks above her ankles.

Seized with ungovernable rage, James raised his arm and brought the riding-crop down on the white skin. O did not flinch. James applied three further blows, each of which lacerated O's body, leaving a burning red weal. O remained motionless and silent throughout the ordeal. Then James threw the crop on to the sofa. He wiped the sweat that was trickling down his forehead. He was breathing heavily and was aware that his face was scarlet. O lowered her head to the floor and lifted her arse higher. 'Have you finished already?' she asked.

James made no reply. 'I'm not one of your thousand-dollar whores,' O said. 'I can take some more.'

James felt more exhausted than he did after making love. 'Don't you feel anything?' he asked, in a weary voice. 'Didn't that hurt?'

'Yes, of course,' O replied, jumping to her feet. 'But it isn't the number of strokes that you receive that indicates your strength; it is the skill that you exhibit in taking them.'

She found the riding-crop, advanced on James, and lashed his chest. He stepped back as the blow landed, but braced himself for more. O lifted the crop again, and brought it down on exactly the same line; the leather bit into James's flesh. He stifled a groan of anger and pain. O raised her arm again, but James caught her wrist, twisted it, and forced her to drop the riding-crop. He drew her towards him, clasped her body against his so that she would feel the strength of his desire, and placed his mouth against hers.

O's lips were unresponsive. 'Goddamn you!' he swore. 'I want you. I'm going to have you.'

He made to kiss her again but she pushed him away.

'Come on, O,' James protested. 'You know you want it too.'

'This is a matter of possession, James,' she said. 'And ownership is a complicated business. You, a powerful man, you should know that.'

'Let's cut out the philosophy,' James shouted. 'No speeches, OK? Just acts. And facts.'

'Is that really all you want?'

'Don't you?' James countered. 'Or is that too scary for you?'

O merely smiled at this provocative challenge. She picked up the riding-crop and replaced it on the table; then she pulled on her tunic as unselfconsciously as if she had been alone. Pembroke stared, fascinated by her body, so slim, so supple, and so self-assured.

'What you are suggesting, James,' she said, 'would be far too simple — beneath our abilities, and perhaps beneath our dignity.'

'So what do you suggest?' he said.

O pondered for a moment. 'Tomorrow night,' she announced, 'I will throw a party in your honour. Everything will be arranged especially for you. Remember that it is necessary to be able to bear mental wounds as well as physical suffering. You will come, won't you? Or does it all sound too scary for you?'

James took her hand and brought it to his lips — the perfect gentleman. 'You bet I'll come,' he said. 'I wouldn't miss this for the world.'

16

That evening there was a heavy atmosphere in the house that O had placed at the disposal of the Pembroke family. The air was stifling; the very walls seemed oppressive, as if they were about to reveal the secrets they had witnessed.

Pierre and Natalie, impeccably dressed as usual in their uniforms, had emphasised the sense of unease by setting the dinner-table for a special occasion. They had laid out silver candelabra, Limoges porcelain, and Baccarat glasses. Pierre had decanted a bottle of Mouton-Rothschild into a cut-glass carafe.

James Pembroke had shut himself in his room as soon as he had returned to the house, and had given instructions that he was not to be disturbed.

'Does that include Madame Pembroke?' Natalie had asked.

'Especially Mrs Pembroke,' he had replied.

For hours he had been making telephone calls, tapping out commands on his computer, and sometimes shouting exclamations that could be heard at the far end of the corridor.

Pierre placed the wine on the table. 'Perhaps we should find out what he's up to,' he suggested to Natalie.

'That's not our job,' the maid replied. 'In any case, I expect it's something to do with Madame.'

Sally Pembroke had returned to the chateau after lunch, accompanied by Karl. The young man had followed her into her bedroom; and when Sally had rung for Natalie, to ask for champagne, the maid had not been allowed into the room.

137

Sally had remained in her room all afternoon. Karl had slipped away at dusk, but Sally did not emerge. When Natalie had knocked at her door, Sally had instructed her to prepare a bath.

'But Madame told me that she would be ready in time for dinner,' Natalie told Pierre.

The butler acknowledged the information with a nod, and said that he too had had a difficult afternoon. Larry had come looking for him.

'Well, well, well,' said Natalie. 'Is that so?'

'Madame O does not appreciate sarcasm in these matters,' Pierre said. 'You know that. You deserve to be punished.'

Natalie imagined herself naked, her wrists shackled above her head. She could almost feel the lashes of the cat-o'-nine-tails, the sailors' whip that seemed to be a favourite of O's.

'Anyway,' Pierre was saying, 'Larry and I had almost no time to ourselves. Jane came looking for her brother.'

Natalie raised her eyebrows in an unspoken question. Pierre shook his head. 'That isn't part of the plan for the time being,' he said. 'Madame O hasn't spoken to me about it. So we merely talked.'

'Talking about it can be just as much fun as doing it,' Natalie said.

'We have fun, as you put it, only when we are ordered to. You will be punished, Natalie.'

Jane entered the dining room. She was wearing a T-shirt and a strawberry pink mini-skirt, and looked like a little girl. She stared in surprise at the damask tablecloth, the ceremonial china, and the silver candlesticks. 'Oh boy!' she said. 'We're hitting the big time tonight. This is real major league!'

'Yes,' Natalie said. 'You should dress for dinner.'

'Are we expecting anyone?'

'I don't believe so,' Pierre said. He pointed to the gilt

138

clock above the fireplace. 'Dinner will be served in a few minutes.'

'I'll only be a moment,' Jane said, on her way to the door.

Natalie followed her. 'I'll come and help you change,' she said.

Jane was conscious that under her skirt her arse and her cunt were completely naked, and she was unable to imagine how she could explain her nudity to the maid. She blushed. 'I . . . I'd rather you didn't,' she stammered.

Natalie knew exactly why the American girl was so embarassed, but she assumed a prim attitude. 'Whatever Mademoiselle wishes,' she declared, haughtily.

Jane turned to her with a look of complete innocence. 'Please understand,' she said, 'it's just that I'm not used to it.'

And that at least, she thought, is quite true.

Three of them — the mother and her two children — met round the big dining table. The father's place was conspicuously empty. They waited some time for him to arrive, but in the end Sally instructed the servants to start serving. Pierre brought in the *foie gras* and toast. They ate in silence, each preoccupied with his or her own thoughts.

Sally, enjoying the firm pink flesh of a lobster, thought about Karl. She summoned up the memory of his long member; of the way he used it to reduce her to nothing more than a thing; and of the way she revelled in it. Sally had read that a good lover should be concerned above all with the reactions of his or her partner. She was at last discovering that for her, not a word of it was true. She was learning to take as much intellectual as physical stimulation from submitting, like a slave, to the desires of a man.

It was only a little while ago that Karl had pulled apart her legs and ordered her to demonstrate how she played with herself. She had refused, protesting that she had not

139

performed such acts since she had been a teenager. Karl, unimpressed, had produced a penknife and opened a blade. He had pressed it against her left breast, pricking the skin with the point. A small drop of blood had appeared. Then he had ordered her again to put on a show for him. *Wank yourself off*, he had said; *I want to see you stuff your fingers right up your cunt.* The words had shocked Sally as much as a slap to the face would have done. Hesitantly, she had placed a hand between her thighs, her fingers seeking the button of flesh hidden among the folds of skin. She had scarcely touched it when she had felt it harden and enlarge. Karl had smoothed the blade of the knife across the underside of her breast; he had touched the knife-point to the tip of her nipple. 'Come on, you whore,' he had said, 'you can do much better than that.'

And Sally had plunged two fingers deeply into the hot, wet folds, leaning backwards and spreading her thighs even wider apart as she caressed herself. Karl's complete indifference had only added to her excitement. Within only a few seconds she had started a shattering crescendo of spasms that had left her drained of energy.

Sally was awoken from her reverie by her daughter. 'This is weird!' Jane said. 'We're all dressed up in evening clothes but there are no guests.'

They all looked at each other disconcertedly, as if suddenly aware of the strangeness of their own behaviour. Sally looked at Natalie; but the maid remained expressionless, even though it had been she who had advised the Pembrokes to dress for dinner. Larry was the first to realise that once again O, operating behind the scenes, had managed to manipulate the family. He gave his mother and sister an ironic look. 'Perhaps we're celebrating something,' he said.

'But what?' Jane asked, thinking of O, and of O's power over her, and of her promise to be permanently available to O.

140

'Larry's right!' Sally suddenly exclaimed; and she summoned the butler. 'Pierre! Bring some champagne!'

The butler withdrew, returning almost immediately with champagne flutes and a bottle in an ice-bucket. 'In this house,' Larry observed, 'the champagne is always ready on the rocks.'

'How come you know that?' asked his sister.

Larry blushed. 'Oh . . . Well,' he mumbled, 'I guess I don't know for sure . . . ' He turned to the butler, who had uncorked the bottle and was pouring the champagne into the glasses. 'But that's so, isn't it, Pierre?'

'It is true that Madame O keeps a good stock of champagne in the house.'

'I guess you know a lot about Madame O and how she does things.'

'Yes, monsieur,' Pierre said. 'Are you perhaps envious?'

Sally interrupted the altercation. 'Let's drink to us,' she said, raising her glass. 'To the family!'

Larry picked up his glass and stared at the bubbles rising through the golden liquid. 'To the Pembrokes,' he said, in a distant voice.

Jane took the last flute of champagne. 'To the family,' she said as she raised it to her lips.

Larry burst out laughing. 'That's one hell of a toast,' he said. 'Anyone would think we were saying our last goodbyes.'

Jane emptied her glass and held it out to Pierre for a refill. 'Whatever makes you think that?'

'This family's not finished yet,' Sally said, 'and nor is any one of us, thank God.'

Larry sought Pierre's eyes, but as usual the butler remained impassive and expressionless. 'It's just that I get the feeling,' Larry explained, 'that things are changing. Like a new page being turned − a new blank sheet in our lives. As if maybe the famous Pembroke family was about to be split up into pieces.'

141

Sally took her son's hand; she found it unpleasantly warm and moist, but she held on to it. 'Your father would never allow that to happen,' she said. 'We know that he loves and respects his family too much for that.'

Larry shook his head. The conversation had taken a turn that he had wanted to avoid. Things were going too far — farther, in any case, than he had ever dared to go with either of his parents. But he was unable to remain silent. Something was compelling him onward, and it wasn't the three mouthfuls of champagne he had consumed. He merely wanted the others to see thing as clearly as he did now.

'To tell you the truth,' he said slowly, 'I think our revered father cares no more about us than about a piece of dogshit on the road.'

Sally did not how to reply. She hoped that Jane would come to her rescue, but the young girl remained silent, a smug smile on her face. Sally fell back on etiquette. 'Watch your language, young man!' she said.

Larry understood his mother's discomfort. 'I'm sorry,' he said. 'I guess I'm tired.'

'I can believe that,' Sally said. 'Seems to me we're all tired. We should get an early night.' She smiled at her daughter. 'Why, I must look a terrible sight!'

She waited for Jane's polite denial, but the girl remained lost in thought. Sally felt somewhat aggrieved. 'I sure need a rest,' she went on. 'I'm invited to a party tomorrow night. I wouldn't want people to think your father ill-treats me!'

Larry stared at a guttering candle-flame. 'That's fine with me,' he said. 'I'm not going to be around tomorrow night either. I've been invited somewhere too.'

'OK with me, too,' Jane said. 'O's asked me over to her place tomorrow. I'll go.'

Sally frowned. Everything seemed strange: the family dispersing, James absent. It was all happening at once, as if someone had planned it; as if someone had decided the

142

fate of the Pembrokes and they were all going along with the plan, without any compulsion. Then Sally thought of Karl, who had told her about the following evening's party, and she was reassured: if there was a plot, it seemed to be for their enjoyment.

She had noticed that her children had changed. At first she had put this down to the travelling, and to being in a foreign country; but she had to face the fact that the changes were more profound than that. Larry she found quite amazing: his shyness had dropped away and he seemed ready to take on the whole world, including his father. Jane, she noticed, was no longer wearing a bra; at first she had regarded this as insignificant — perhaps a passing fashion — but now she saw it as part of a bid for freedom. She was careful not to criticise, however; if she had been her daughter's age, and sure of her bosom, she would have done the same.

Having considered her children, Sally pushed back her chair and stood up. 'James will sure be surprised to find himself dining alone,' she said.

Larry shrugged. 'Perhaps we should tell him.'

'Forget it,' Jane said. 'When he finally comes down Pierre can tell him that we're all busy. That'll do.'

Larry whistled. 'Wow! This is some revolution that's going on in the Pembroke palace.'

Sally poured herself a full glass of champagne. 'Maybe so,' she said. 'But I won't drink to it. I don't see that it's anything to celebrate.'

She swallowed the contents of the glass, which she then threw over her shoulder. It shattered on the floor at the feet of Natalie, who did not even flinch. Brother and sister, staring open-mouthed in astonishment, failed to respond when their mother wished them goodnight. With a gait that she would have liked to appear more assured than it was, Sally left the dining room.

Larry exchanged a glance with his sister. 'Strange woman, that Sally Pembroke,' he said.

'Don't joke about it,' Jane replied.

'You don't reckon that everything'll work out fine in the end?'

'I just don't know,' Jane said. She looked towards the two servants, as silent and unmoving as ever. Their presence was beginning to annoy her. She lowered her voice. 'I'm scared,' she confided to her brother.

Larry made no reply. Once again his sister had said out loud something that he had not dared to admit. But he found his fear exciting.

Jane turned to Natalie and pointed at the broken glass. 'Don't you think you ought to clear that up?'

With great deliberation Natalie positioned herself with her back to Jane before bending down to collect the shards of glass. As the short black skirt lifted stiffly to jut almost horizontally from the maid's waist, Jane could see that between stocking tops and suspender belt Natalie, too, was completely naked.

17

The walls of the room were white-washed; the sunlight was harsh. There were no chairs, no bed, not even a carpet to cover the red-tiled floor.

Jane turned to O. She was bursting with questions, the most important of which was *Where are you taking me?* — but she knew it would be futile to ask. She would not receive an answer.

That afternoon, the day after the ceremonial dinner, Jane had been getting ready for her visit to O's lodge when O herself had appeared in the room. Jane had been naked, about to try on a short sleeveless dress. She had jumped in surprise, and had tried to cover herself; which was ridiculous, she had realised immediately, because O had seen her body before, had caressed her, and had witnessed her being offered for the satisfaction of various men.

'Remember,' O had said, 'when you least expect me . . .'

Jane had always known what lay behind O's invitation; and in spite of the fear that was beginning to twist in her entrails, she had accepted it. She had started to look for something to wear. O had pointed to the dress. 'That one will do,' O had said. 'Let us not waste time.'

Jane had obeyed. As they left the chateau Jane had realised that O had arrived on foot. O had set off across the park. 'Where are we going?' Jane had asked. 'Is it very near?' O did not bother to reprimand her for her curiosity.

They had passed the carp pool and had entered the woods. O had taken a path that was bordered with oaks and poplars, beneath which the undergrowth of brambles was thick with berries. Jane had wanted to linger there, and to breathe in the scents of moss and leaves; but O had urged her to hurry onwards, and it had seemed to Jane that the buzzing of the insects had become louder and more threatening.

They had reached a little iron gate that O had opened with a key. Beyond the gate Jane had found herself standing in front of a house which was very similar to the house to which she had been taken by Sir Stephen. As if dreaming, Jane had found that she could not be sure whether or not it was the same house. There had seemed to be differences between the two, and the fact that she had seen one of them at night and the other by day had nothing to do with her confusion. It had been rather as if the same elements − the stone blocks, the copper beech hedges, the angles of the roof − had been subtly modified from one building to the other.

O had given Jane no time for a deeper analysis of her surroundings. She had led Jane to a door of varnished wood into which a spy-hole had been set, and had rung the bell. The door had been opened by a young girl, with carmine lips and purple eyes, wearing a long black dress; she had stood aside to let them in and had then closed the door behind them. Jane had felt as if she had been entering a prison. Silently, the girl had gestured for them to follow her. Jane had noticed how the sheer black material of the dress had clung to the girl's figure, even though the garment was slit to the waist at the back and sides, revealing the girl's naked body with each step that she took. Jane had caught several glimpses of the pale skin at the tops of the girl's thighs, and she had been sure that she had seen whip-marks there.

Jane had been seized with terror. She had been overcome by a sudden urge to turn round and flee; but O had grasped her wrists and pulled her onwards. They had passed through corridors separated by heavy doors, each of which had been unlocked and then secured behind them by the girl. And thus they had arrived in the white-washed room, where they had finally stopped.

Jane was still wondering whether she was in a dream — or perhaps a nightmare. She thought that if she could only make the effort she would wake up.

As if reading her thoughts, O turned to reassure her. 'You don't need to try to understand what happens now. You don't have to ask questions. You are here because, deep down, it is in your nature. There is nothing you can do about it, in the end.' She smiled. 'You can try to find explanations, of course,' she added, 'but explanations are worthless.'

All the same, Jane wanted to carry on talking. It felt good to be able to listen to O's serious, husky voice. 'O,' she said, 'I can sense that we're alike, you and I. We recognised each other at first sight, didn't we?'

O laughed. 'If you mean that you're here because of me and for my enjoyment, I agree with you. But you have always known that.'

'I know.'

O thrust her hands under the material of Jane's dress and gripped the girl's nipples, pulling her forwards. Jane felt her heart leap; her legs felt weak. She lifted her face towards O, who kissed her lips and murmured: 'You are mine, Jane.'

Then she pushed the girl away. 'Now be quiet. We are going to prepare you.'

The girl in black undid Jane's dress and let it fall to the floor. Jane was now completely naked. The girl opened a cupboard in the wall and took out two leather bracelets and a metal collar. Jane had to protest. 'You're not going to give me to some more of your friends?'

'That is not for you to decide. For the moment, we are simply getting you ready. I enjoy ritual.'

All hope evaporated. Jane tried to cling to O. 'No, please,' she moaned, 'I beg you, no. It's so humiliating.'

'So much for your obedience,' said O, icily; and she slapped Jane's face, twice, making her reel from side to side. The girl in black stood behind her and supported her; and then, as Jane's sobs quietened, the girl started to kiss her softly on the neck and shoulders. The girl then slid round Jane, and took a nipple in her mouth, sucking gently, and then licking round the edge of the aureole, and then giving a little bite, and then sucking again. Jane felt her breasts begin to swell with pleasure; her sex became wet with desire. The girl in black knelt, her hands remaining on Jane's breasts, stroking and pinching, while her lips ran up Jane's thighs, and then into the neat triangle of golden hair. Her tongue quested along the furrow, parted Jane's secret lips, and found the pleasure-button, which was then remorselessly sucked, licked and nibbled. Jane, overwhelmed by the sensations rippling up through her body, could only offer herself up to them, throwing her head back and pushing her sex forward. O came to stand behind her, fondling her breasts and kissing her face and mouth. The girl in black continued to tongue Jane's sex, and now used her hands to grip Jane's buttocks, at the same time inserting a finger into the rear passage. Jane squirmed with delight, and tried to turn towards O to return her caresses; but O held her firmly, and placing a hand on the back of the head of the girl in black she pushed her face hard against Jane's wet cunt. Jane was penetrated by a finger and by a tongue, and above all she was encircled by O's arms and surrounded by O's perfume.

With a series of cries and shudders, Jane reached her climax. Only when the last spasm had receded did O release her grip on the head of the girl in black, allowing her to slide to the floor and then leave the room, her face and mouth wet with Jane's juices. O stood in front of Jane, who opened her eyes to find herself facing her friend's emerald-green gaze; a gaze that held her while the door opened again to admit a masked man. The tunic that was his only garment fell open at the front; in his hand he held a whip. He seized Jane by the waist and pulled her towards the wall in which, Jane had noticed, iron rings were set. He clicked the leather bracelets about her wrists, and fastened the metal collar round her neck. O handed him three lengths of chain, each of which had a slip-catch at both ends. Within seconds Jane was shackled to the rings in the wall, her arms wide apart. She could step from side to side, but she was obliged to remain standing, and she could not lower her arms to cover her body.

For a few moments O and the masked man watched Jane as she explored the limits of her movements, pulling on the rings and rattling the chains; and then O indicated that the man should proceed. He stepped forward and raised the whip.

It was a relatively mild instrument of punishment, being small and light; but it had six thin strands of leather, each tipped with a knot, and it hissed ferociously through the air as it rose and fell. After the first lash, across her stomach, Jane knew that the whip would not cause her serious harm; but the pain was sharp and biting, and she could not restrain her yelps and screams and her futile twisting and turning. At first the masked man concentrated on her stomach, moving on to her hips and thighs; then, just as Jane thought he had finished, he attacked her breasts with renewed vigour. Jane wept now, her tears blinding her, her cries reduced to sobs and whimpers. She caught glimpses of O, her green eyes watching every blow fall; she caught glimpses of the man's member, rigidly protruding from his tunic. At last she stopped struggling and stood still, defeated, her head bowed and tears streaming down her face; and the masked man paused briefly, and then unleashed a storm of vicious blows on the unmoving targets of her breasts.

O instructed the man to stop, and stepped forward to examine the results of the flogging. Her cool fingers ran across the tracery of whip-marks that criss-crossed Jane's bosom. The man pointed interrogatively, and O nodded her agreement; whereupon the man started to release the chains from Jane's wrists and neck.

Freed from her shackles, Jane shook herself and stretched; but the man then took her arms and forced her to her knees. The girl in black scurried back into the room and knelt behind Jane, holding her wrists together with one hand while with the other she parted Jane's thighs and fingered her sex and the ring of her anus. The masked man, meanwhile, stood in front of Jane, grabbed her hair, lifted her head, and stuffed his tumescent organ into her mouth. Jane choked at first, but then shaped her lips round the stiff cylinder. The man thrust to and fro, careless of Jane's muffled cries. The girl in black had worked her fingers and thumb deeply into Jane from two directions, and when she leant forward and started to kiss the nape of Jane's neck, Jane felt waves of pleasure begin to overcome the discomfort of the man's invasion of her mouth. And then her lower lip detected a trembling at the base of the man's pole of flesh, which seemed to expand to fill her mouth; and his sperm exploded into her throat. Jane sucked hard, dissolving the glutinous fluid with her saliva before swallowing it. As the man withdrew his member, she looked up at him with a tear-dimmed smile.

This served only to enrage the man. 'So you think you've won, do you?' he snarled. 'It's all been too easy for you, Jane.' And Jane watched in horror as he retrieved his whip and raised it into the air.

He flogged her mercilessly, and without care or finesse. She ran, crawled, rolled about the room, attempting to escape the flailing tails of leather; but he followed her, herded her into a corner, and rained blows upon her until she was hysterically begging for mercy. And then, without another word, he left the room.

O looked down at Jane; then knelt beside her, parted her thighs, and her lowered her head to the girl's blonde triangle. O's mouth kissed Jane's lower lips; O's tongue entered Jane's sex, and found it dripping. The girl in black lay down behind Jane; buried her face between Jane's buttocks; and insinuated her tongue into the tight orifice there.

Penetrated simultaneously by two tongues, Jane trembled; arched her body; and released a long shriek of ecstasy.

The girl in black left the room. O helped Jane to her feet, and then took from the cupboard a purple dress with vents at the sides and back. O answered the questions that Jane was too terrified to ask.

'Truth is to be found in sex; in despair; and in going to extremes. In everything that takes you to your limits, even if you don't know that you want to be taken there.'

Jane looked at the leather bracelets that were still fastened round her wrists. O shook her head. 'You must keep them on,' she said. 'We are not yet at the end of the road.' She helped Jane to put on a pair of velvet slippers that matched the dress. 'Everybody has dreams,' she went on, 'in an imaginary universe; these are called fantasies. Very few people are able to turn them into reality; those who succeed have access to worlds that are unknown to the rest of humanity. They have a unique knowledge; a knowledge that they cannot share with others, because it can be communicated only by experience.'

Jane nodded; she understood what O had told her. She tried to wipe her eyes, to tidy up the eyeshadow that had run down her cheeks; but O stopped her. 'You can wash later,' O said. 'From time to time it's good for you to live with your own dirt.'

'O,' Jane said, reflectively, 'I would never have believed that I would be able to tolerate what I've just been through.'

151

'We prepared you for it,' O said. 'Not just by bringing you here, but mentally. Don't forget that everything that has happened to you has happened because you wanted it. That first evening, you had only to say no to Sir Stephen; everything would have stopped, and you would have been taken straight home.'

'But I could have cracked under the pressure! At any time!'

O looked at her and said gravely: 'You? Never. You were born for this.'

'Does that mean I'll turn out like you?'

O thought before replying. 'You can, if you want to.'

'I want to.'

Without replying, O made to leave the room. Jane started to follow her, but O turned round. 'Stay here,' she ordered. 'People want to carry on watching you.'

And Jane realised that behind the white walls were hidden eyes that had missed nothing that had been done to her — eyes that had seen her chained, whipped, humiliated, violated and, worst of all, had seen her come.

She thought at first that she would be plunged into shame and despair; and she was surprised to find that instead she felt a strange sense of pride — and, beyond that, a form of happiness.

18

Ginsberg was short and balding; he had a pointed beard and a permanently preoccupied expression. Clutching a worn leather attaché case he dashed into the arrival lounge at Roissy airport and immediately recognised James Pembroke, who was waiting for him. He went up to his boss, shook his outstretched hand, and fell into step beside him.

'Glad to have you along,' James said. 'I can promise you one thing: you won't be bored.'

The little man nodded in agreement. He had a great deal of respect for James Pembroke, and almost as much mistrust of him. He had no illusions: he knew that as long as he was useful, the tycoon would treat him well; but when Pembroke found another Ginsberg – younger, more dynamic, better informed – the obsolete model would be out, with a handshake considerably less golden than he felt he deserved.

James approved of Ginsberg's insight. He was used to betraying people as much as to being betrayed, and he liked his staff to have no illusions about him. It saved time.

When they were seated in the back of the limousine, James offered Ginsberg a Romeo y Julieta. Ginsberg declined, but James lit a cigar for himself. 'This your first time in Paris?' he asked.

'First time for forty years,' Ginsberg replied.

'You were here after the war?'

'I was nine.'

James didn't pursue the subject. 'It's a city of surprises,' he said from within a cloud of smoke. 'You'll find out. You learn a whole pile of stuff here. About other people . . . about yourself . . . '

'I just hope I get time to visit the Louvre'

Ash from James's cigar fell on to the carpet. Ginsberg was obviously useful for figures and share dealings and not much else. James Pembroke had no time to spare for the Mona Lisa.

For once Carel's eyes were not fixed on Gina's sumptuous bosom. He didn't feel his usual urge to stick his hand up her black leather skirt. But then, today she had just brought him some particularly important news.

'The meeting with Monsieur Pembroke has been confirmed, monsieur. You are expected at the Morton Bank.'

'When?'

Gina leant towards him, and he could see that her breasts were suntanned all over. He wondered where she spent her weekends. 'Immediately, monsieur,' she said. 'I've phoned for the car to take you.'

'Cancel it,' Carel ordered.

She looked surprised. He took her hand. 'I'll take a cab,' he explained. 'And tell me, Gina – on Saturday . . . '

He let the sentence hang in the air. The girl freed her hand from his. 'Saturday, monsieur?'

'Nothing, nothing,' he said, picking up his briefcase and heading towards the door. 'And remember now: not a word of this to anyone. Not even Botterweg. This meeting at the Morton Bank is absolutely confidential.'

'Of course, monsieur,' Gina said; and Carel left, wondering, as he did every day, why he never had the courage to ask her for a date.

Botterweg answered the telephone. As he had expected, the call was from Morton, the banker. 'I'm just leaving,' he said. 'I'll be there in about ten minutes.' And, although he knew it was a tactical error he couldn't help adding: 'You see? It's all going according to plan. Pembroke's as harmless as a puppy.' He laughed complacently. 'No, don't worry — I won't be late. Not on a day like this. I've waited a long time for today.'

He replaced the receiver and pulled on his jacket. As he left he glanced into the mirror: club tie, grey flannel suit, blue shirt; relaxed and yet sober. He was pleased with himself. 'Daniel Botterweg,' he repeated to himself, 'Chairman and Managing Director of Capitol Industries.'

Basically, he thought to himself, it was very straightforward. You simply had to be more bloody-minded than the opposition.

The walls were faced with marble, the terrace overlooked the Eiffel Tower, there was a swimming pool on the roof. Morton's hair was plastered flat against his skull, and he was so fat that his shirt, although made to measure, gaped open across his belly and revealed his navel. His hand outstretched in greeting, he lumbered towards James Pembroke.

'I thought it best to see you here, in my Paris apartment. More intimate.'

'Is that what you call it,' James said. 'My guess is you're trying to impress me. And I agree that it's smart to put on a show — just so long as what's on display really is your own.'

'And what exactly do you mean by that?' Morton growled.

'This here is Ginsberg — one of my most valued advisers. He knows everything there is to know. Like for instance that you rent these three hundred square metres from Sheikh Al Fayed — by the week.'

'That's quite ridiculous,' Morton spat.

James turned to his sidekick. 'Ginsberg, give me the photocopy of Morton's cheque.'

155

Ginsberg started to open his attaché case. 'That won't be necessary,' Morton said hurriedly. 'You have won, Pembroke — thus far, at any rate. This proves nothing about the state of my finances. In fact, as you know exactly how much this bijoux little residence costs me, you can work out for yourselves how much I'm worth.'

He led them along the length of the swimming pool and into a drawing room furnished with leather-covered armchairs and *chaises longues*. A bottle of champagne stood waiting in an ice-bucket.

James dropped into one of the armchairs. Morton sat opposite him. Ginsberg occupied a sofa, his attaché case open beside him.

'Let's talk straight,' James said. 'I've made enquiries; I'll bet you have too. Capitol represents a considerable amount of money. I can't believe that you're prepared to risk that kind of cash.' He waved his arm in a gesture that took in the swimming pool, the terrace, and the Eiffel Tower beyond the picture window. 'And this set-up doesn't impress me, Morton. You should come and see my place in Houston.'

Morton smiled and brushed a hand across his flattened hair. 'You're a powerful man, Pembroke,' he said, 'but you're rather unsubtle. You assume that everyone wants to be your rival. But I assure you, that isn't my intention.'

'Glad to hear it. Are the contracts ready?'

'We're only waiting for Botterweg,' Morton said.

Ginsberg glanced at his watch. 'He's on his way now,' he said.

At that moment a doorbell rang. Morton looked at Pembroke's adviser in alarm. 'You really do know everything,' he gasped.

'It's my job,' Ginsberg replied.

'And now we have to move very fast, Morton,' James said, rising to his feet. 'Let's talk!'

156

The meeting started a little later, in a room furnished in royal blue. An antique tapestry occupied the whole of one wall; on the opposite wall a Picasso and a Mondrian were on display. James studied them knowledgeably. 'Very nice pieces,' he commented.

'From Sotheby's last sale of moderns,' Ginsberg added.

'Are you also a connoisseur of art?' Morton asked.

James replied for both of them. 'We're interested in anything that can be bought and sold.'

Botterweg was the first to take a seat; he positioned himself at the head of the marble table. Here, too, a bottle of champagne was waiting in an ice-bucket, and alongside it a tray of glasses.

'I suggest that we start the proceedings,' Botterweg announced.

'In a hurry, Botterweg?' James said.

'I must admit that I didn't expect to find you here,' Botterweg said. He turned to Morton. 'Is there a problem?'

It was Ginsberg who replied. 'Not at all, Mr Botterweg. We have the situation under control.'

Botterweg attempted to conceal his disquiet. 'I am glad to make your acquaintance, Monsieur Ginsberg. You have a reputation in financial circles.'

Ginsberg accepted the compliment with a smile. 'We were only waiting for you to see the documents being signed.' At a sign from Pembroke, he took from his attaché case a folder of contracts. He perched a pair of gold-rimmed spectacles on his nose and declared: 'Mr Morton has agreed to buy those shares in Capitol Industries that we currently hold. We have agreed on a price of one hundred and twenty dollars a share. Officially, none of us knows for whom Mr Morton is acting; we don't know who is behind the deal and who will benefit from it. But perhaps each of us has an inkling of the truth.'

Botterweg was very pleased with Ginsberg's little speech.

157

He grinned in approval. Ginsberg placed the documents on the marble table and slid them towards Pembroke and Morton, each of whom produced a large fountain pen from his jacket pocket. As they initialled the pages, Botterweg was unable to conceal his excitement. When the last page had been signed, he picked up his briefcase and passed it to Pembroke; James opened the case, glanced at the contents, and then closed it with an expression of disgust. He spun the combination locks before handing the case to Ginsberg. 'Have this destroyed,' he said, 'as soon as we're finished here.'

Botterweg's mouth was dry. 'I need a drink. I hope you'll join me. This is a great day for Daniel Botterweg.'

Morton indicated that the champagne was ready. Botterweg popped the cork and poured the wine into the glasses. James raised his glass. 'I propose a toast,' he said in a serious voice.

At that moment there was a knock on the door. 'Yes?' Morton barked.

A secretary appeared in the doorway. 'Monsieur Carel is here,' she whispered to Morton.

'Carel?' Morton was surprised.

'He says he has an appointment with you,' the secretary said.

Botterweg slammed his glass on to the table so violently that the stem broke. Champagne flowed across the table and dripped on to his trousers. He jumped to his feet and dabbed at himself with a handkerchief while staring at each of those present in turn. 'Which of you asked him to come here?' he demanded.

'I did,' James replied. 'I guess I thought it would put the cap on your victory if Carel were here too. We'll see if he's a good loser.'

Botterweg thumped his fist on the table. 'There are certain matters, Pembroke, that should remain strictly private.'

158

'It reassures me to hear you say that,' James sneered.

Botterweg glared. 'I hope we understand each other, Pembroke.'

James refused to pursue the conversation. He turned to the secretary. 'Tell Mr Carel to come in.'

Henri Carel entered the room unconcernedly, but stopped in surprise when he saw that both Pembroke and Botterweg were present. His hand went instinctively to his pocket, as if he had a concealed weapon. James stood up and approached him.

'Glad to see you, Carel. You got here just in time. Botterweg is about to propose a toast. I guess you'll want to raise a glass along with us.'

Carel frowned. He looked like a man who was sure he'd fallen into a trap. 'Pembroke,' he said, 'could you tell me what Daniel is doing here? What's this all about?'

James went back to his armchair and flopped into it. He made an expansive gesture towards Botterweg, who had managed to resume his confident air. 'Your pal Daniel can explain the whole thing,' James said.

In a voice that was rather too emphatic, Botterweg said: 'Henri, you know that we have our differences on the subject of the management of Capitol. In the interests of the company, and regardless of what it will cost me, I thought it best for me to take control.'

Carel was incredulous. 'Control?'

'We have purchased the shares in the company that Monsieur Pembroke had amassed.'

'We?' Carel demanded. 'Who is this "we"?'

Botterweg brought his hand to his face in an attempt to conceal his triumphant satisfaction. Real men of power, he told himself, remain impassive whatever the circumstances. 'Actually, it's me,' he said, as calmly as he could. 'I appointed the Morton bank to act as an intermediary.'

Carel lost his temper. 'You miserable little bastard!' he

159

yelled, advancing on Botterweg, who cowered in his chair. 'I'll make you pay for this!' He spun round to face Morton. 'And that goes for you, too.'

The banker lit a cigar. 'If I were you, Carel,' he said, 'I'd watch my language. And I'd avoid jumping to conclusions.'

Carel turned away in disgust. He pointed at Pembroke. 'As for you, Pembroke — what on earth induced you to deal with this little mediocrity? If you wanted to dispose of your interest in Capitol you could have approached me.'

'Botterweg did me a good turn,' James said. 'He let me in your plans to compromise me — '

Botterweg gave Carel no time to explain whose idea it had been to involve the Pembrokes in a scandal. 'I knew,' he broke in, 'that Pembroke had no desire to keep the Capitol shares for himself. I informed him that he and his family would be exposed to certain risks unless he agreed to sell his shareholding to me. Morton conducted the financial negotiations; but the real buyer is me. You're finished, Henri.'

Carel leant against the wall. He looked at each of the four seated men in turn. 'Daniel,' he said thoughtfully, 'I cannot believe that Morton is backing you. His is a serious banking operation.'

'Why the hell shouldn't they?' Botterweg replied vehemently. 'They know me. They understand me. They know that I can run Capitol a damn sight more competently than you. You lack vision, Carel. The company deserves better than to have a nonentity like you in charge.'

Carel looked revolted. 'You're showing your true colours at last, Daniel.' He turned to Morton. 'You have really bought the shares?'

'Oh yes.'

'I'll put it another way: who owns the shares now?'

It was Ginsberg who answered. 'The Morton bank.'

160

Carel looked at Ginsberg and then at Pembroke. He turned back to Morton, and his eyes came to rest on Botterweg. There was something fishy about the whole business. 'So who put up the money?' he asked.

Botterweg shrugged. 'I told you: the bank.'

Carel thought about this for a moment; and then he started to laugh quietly. Pembroke, Morton and Ginsberg watched him with interest. Botterweg felt beads of sweat break out on his forehead; the others shared a tacit understanding that unnerved him.

Carel faced Morton again. 'One more question,' he said. 'Morton, did your bank put up the finance for this deal?'

'No,' the banker said.

Botterweg swore. Carel gave him a pitying look. 'Poor old Daniel,' he sighed. 'You're not worth a centime more than I am. We've both been had. Pembroke's tricked us all. He put up the money, don't you see? He has sold his shares to himself, using Morton as an intermediary. I wouldn't be surprised if he's used the transaction to make some profit along the way.'

Botterweg seemed crushed by this revelation. He sat, dazed, for several seconds. Then he pushed back his chair so violently that it fell backwards to the floor. 'You've swindled me, Pembroke,' he shrieked, shaking his fist. 'I'll get even with you!'

James drained his glass and summoned Ginsberg to refill it. 'Don't try to threaten me, Botterweg,' he said, his voice full of contempt. 'I know you're as treacherous as a snake; don't start acting stupid, too.' His voice rose to a roar. 'Now get out. You're all through here. You're washed up. Nobody has ever gotten away with blackmailing me. Just be grateful you're getting out of this with your skin intact.'

Carel was enjoying the scene. Botterweg strode out in silent fury and slammed the door. 'Gentlemen,' Carel said, 'I will also take my leave.'

He went towards the door, but Ginsberg called out to him. 'If I were you, Carel, I'd hang on in for a while.'

Carel shook his head like a teacher addressing a stubborn pupil. 'No, Ginsberg, please don't insist. I understand the situation. Pembroke has won. Now he is going to ask me to continue as Chairman, to maintain continuity and reassure the other shareholders. But in six months he will of course get rid of me.'

James smiled. 'You're not dumb,' he said, approvingly. 'And you know you have to accept that offer. You have no choice. It's the only way you can get out of this with your hands clean.'

Carel opened the door. From the threshold, he said: 'So you know my answer. You're right, I have no choice. I'm going back to the office. I'll await your instructions.'

The door closed. The three remaining men sat in silence for a few moments. Morton considered that although he had not been hoaxed, he had nonetheless been manipulated. Up until a few minutes previously even he had not been sure whose funds he had been using to purchase Pembroke's Capitol shareholding. However, a bank can always benefit from handling a large sum, even if it is held only briefly; and a banker must be prepared to be flexible. Morton therefore decided that instead of embarking on recriminations, he would behave as if he were Pembroke's associate. He drew on his cigar and adopted a worried expression that emphasised his triple chin. 'What are you going to do about Botterweg?' he asked.

'What do you care what happens to him?'

Morton waved his arm, as if sweeping away Botterweg and any suggestion that he might defend his former ally. Pembroke and Ginsberg understood the gesture and exchanged glances: they had expected the banker to come over to the stronger side. This final act of treachery came as no surprise to them. James looked at his watch and then

162

gazed at the Eiffel Tower. 'I don't give a damn about Botterweg,' he said in a flat tone.

Morton, however, had worries of his own concerning Botterweg's anger. 'You've driven him into a corner,' he insisted. 'Men are like animals: when they have nothing to lose, they are dangerous.'

James stood up and wandered to the window. He watched a barge floating on the sparkling water of the Seine. 'It's all fixed up,' he said. 'I've left instructions. Botterweg will be offered a senior position in another company. Of course,' he went on, 'he'll never know that the job's down to me. So he'll still be useful to us.'

Ginsberg replaced the contracts in his attaché case. 'OK,' he said with finality, 'everything's sewn up.'

'Not everything,' James said. 'There is one person I still have to deal with.'

He marched out of the room, leaving Morton and Ginsberg speechless.

19

James had dressed in an evening suit, and was ready to follow up O's invitation. He sat on his bed and studied, one last time, the dossier that Ginsberg had compiled on the woman. He had to admit that he was up against a formidable adversary. He sighed, stood up, and threw the papers on to the fire that was burning in the grate.

When he turned round, she was there beside him, in a moire silk dress. O was standing in his bedroom, a faint smile on her lips. James looked at the door: he was sure that he had locked it. 'How did you get in here?' he demanded.

'I have my methods.'

'What does that mean?'

'I have secrets, if you like. Shall we go?'

'Are we going far?'

'Only a few steps,' O said. James started to check over his clothing. 'We don't even have to leave the house,' she added.

'Is that so?' James said sarcastically. 'Is that the band I can hear playing already?'

'Don't waste words,' O said. 'Follow me.'

She touched part of the wooden panelling, and a door, hidden in the wall, swung open. James gave a whistle of surprise, and followed her. She led him into a dark corridor that ended in a small room furnished with a sofa, a low table and an armchair. Pulling aside a picture that was hanging on the wall, she revealed two small peep-holes that allowed a view of everything that went on in the neighbouring room.

'Look!' she said; but James already knew that the next

room was his wife's bedroom. He stared through the holes at the unmade bed and the clothes scattered all over the carpet.

'Let's get on,' he said at last.

O pressed a button that was concealed behind the sofa; almost noiselessly the entire room began to descend. It was, in fact, a large lift. When it stopped, O opened a low door and proceeded along passages and up and down staircases until she stopped in a bare white-walled room. James could hear the muffled sounds of voices, tinkling glasses, and background music. 'We have arrived,' O said.

Following O, James had been unable to take his eyes off her buttocks, undulating under the thin silk of her dress. Now he remembered details that Ginsberg had collected in his report, and suddenly he felt nervous. James Pembroke, the millionaire moral crusader, was about to be plunged into the midst of the temptations that he had spent his life denouncing.

'Here,' O told him, 'guests are not introduced to each other. You are free to speak to anyone; but you will receive a reply only if I allow it. Everyone here is my guest, and these are the rules of my house.'

James nodded. 'There is one more thing,' O said. 'You must promise that under no circumstances will you interfere with, or try to prevent, anything that you may see or hear. Can you manage that?'

'OK,' James succeeded in saying, 'I swear it. I swear to God.'

The walls of the room were draped in black. All the chairs and sofas were covered in black velvet. The tables were made of ebony. The only light came from candles, and from the logs burning in the fireplace.

About a dozen men were there, drinking scotch or champagne, chatting or reading newspapers. They were waited on by uniformed servants. James saw that the members of this strange club were dressed in two strikingly different ways: some, like him, were wearing dinner jackets; others were wearing nothing but kimonos or tunics that opened to reveal that they were otherwise naked.

There was a greater number of women, but they were, in the main, ignored by the men. Some had their wrists secured behind their backs; others, on leashes, knelt next to the chairs in which their masters sat. Every one wore leather bracelets and a metal collar studded with rings.

James and O passed unremarked across the room. The men ignored them; and the rule of the establishment was that the women were to keep their eyes cast downward.

O led James to a table across which a man with grey hair and eyes — Sir Stephen — was deep in conversation with a younger man. 'I am prepared to bet,' Sir Stephen was saying, 'that you could not tell the difference.'

The other man, impeccably dressed in an evening suit, was prepared to dispute the point. 'I have observed the faces of many women at the moment of climax,' he said. 'I assure you I can recognise the transformation that occurs.'

'And I,' Sir Stephen replied, 'have observed the faces of many women while they have been receiving a whipping. The expression is identical to that of a woman having an orgasm. There is no detectable difference. During both experiences a woman loses her identity.'

A man with fair hair butted in. 'This is interesting. Let's have a wager on it.' Others joined in, and it was decided that an experiment was required.

Sir Stephen pointed to a dark-haired girl with small breasts, slim hips, and large round eyes. 'This one will do,' he said, and turned to his younger companion. 'You choose the other.'

The young man cast his eyes across the twenty or so women in the room. He stopped when he saw a buxom

166

blonde, her wrists tied together, her buttocks showing the faded stripes of a whip.

Sir Stephen had the two chosen women chained loosely to the wall. Then he instructed the servants to stand in a line in front of them, so that a wall of bodies hid the women from the rest of the room. Finally, the two women were made to push their heads forward, between the thighs of the footmen immediately in front of them, so that their faces were now visible and so that they would not be able to move.

Sir Stephen beckoned to the young man. 'Come over here,' he said. 'Take a chair, make yourself comfortable. You can see their faces clearly from here. You have to be close enough to detect the slightest changes in their expressions.'

The young man strolled across the room and sat down. Sir Stephen had still not finished. 'You will have to plug your ears, of course,' he mused. 'If you can hear their cries and shouts, the experiment will be useless.'

'I know!' the young man said. He summoned a servant. 'Bring me a personal stereo, with earphones. I'll play music at full volume.'

Within minutes the cassette player had arrived. The young man placed the earphones on his head. 'Schubert seems to me to be appropriate,' he said.

'It's entirely up to you,' Sir Stephen replied; but the young man seemed unable to hear his words. Sir Stephen, determined to ensure that the experiment should succeed, summoned a dark-skinned, doe-eyed girl for one final test. He made her kneel behind the young man's chair and, clutching a handful of her black curls, he asked two of the men to pluck some of the long glossy hairs from her labia and from close to her anus. He was soon rewarded with a cacophony of screams and shrieks — none of which, it appeared, could be heard by the young man, who was sitting

167

cross-legged and swinging his foot in time with the music that filled his ears.

Sir Stephen released the girl and turned to his audience. 'Which of you would like to take part in the experiment?' he asked.

The fair-haired man opened his tunic to reveal a member that was thin, but long and very evidently ready for action. An elderly man with a gnarled body picked up a slender whip. They nodded to Sir Stephen and disappeared behind the wall of servants.

Sir Stephen stood in front of the young man and raised his eyebrows questioningly. The young man raised a hand: he was not quite ready. He beckoned to the nearest woman, a petite redhead with short curly hair and a wide-eyed, freckled face. She knelt between his legs, extricated his rapidly-stiffening organ, and held it between her cool white hands as she formed her mouth into a perfect circle to accommodate it. She started to suck and lick greedily.

Sir Stephen clapped his hands. 'The penetration must start first,' he announced. 'Pleasure comes more slowly than pain.' And in a harsher voice he added: 'I order you all to watch!' All round the room, the women lifted their heads.

Sir Stephen remained standing in front of the young man so that he should not see that the fair-haired man was already at work on the dark-haired girl. Unseen behind the human wall, the girl's vagina was moistly receiving a long, thin penis; her anal sphincter was tightly clenched round two fingers; her clitoris was being massaged in circular movements. The spectators, who could see only her face, watched appreciatively as she gasped, pursed her lips, squeezed her eyes shut and then opened them wide. When Sir Stephen judged that her orgasm was approaching, he said: 'Now! Start whipping the other one!' — and, when he thought that the two women had reached an equal level of pleasure and pain, he stood aside to let the young man see their faces.

Behind the wall of servants, the old man was flogging the blonde's plump buttocks with surprising energy. He stood behind her, aiming always at her sex and the tops of her thighs, catching her with the return strokes as well as with the forehand lashes.

From in front, it could be seen that her eyes were unfocused and filled with tears, that her breath was harsh and panting, that her lips were writhing — in short, that she was in the grip of overwhelming emotions.

But by now the dark girl was ravaged with pleasure, her body wracked with spasms and her face contorted. She gave a final shuddering cry as she reached her climax, and then her head dropped and she was still. Almost simultaneously the blonde, overcome with pain and exhaustion, collapsed to the floor. And at the same time the young man, who had been idly stroking the titian curls that were moving between his thighs, plunged deeply into the red-head's obedient mouth and spurted his seed into her throat.

'Well?' Sir Stephen asked.

There was a long silence. The young man removed the earphones from his head and looked from the blonde's tear-stained face to the glazed eyes of the brunette. 'Do you know,' he finally admitted, 'I really can't say which has been whipped and which has been fucked!'

The scene was over. Without waiting for instruction, all the women lowered their eyes. The men resumed their seats and called for more drinks. The two girls who had been the instruments of the experiment remained chained to the wall. O put a hand on James's arm. He had missed nothing of the entertainment. 'And what about you, James?' she said. 'Could you have judged which was which?'

'No,' he admitted, 'I reckon not. But I guess I could if I knew the ladies in question.'

O was impatient with his answer. 'That's absurd. Sexual pleasure and pain reduce human beings to their most primitive core. At the extremes they consist of nothing but these two elements: pleasure and pain.'

James glared wrathfully at this assembly of men and women who seemed determined to complicate matters which he regarded as essentially simple. He decided on a frontal assault. 'Just tell me this,' he growled at O: 'why have you brought me here? And what's your plan?'

'My plan? Why, to seduce you, of course.'

James was unable to conceal his impatience. O noticed his irritation. 'If you were an ordinary man,' she explained, 'I could have approached you like an ordinary woman: I could have let you glimpse my knees, and then a thigh, and then down the front of a low-cut dress — and so on. But you deserve better than that; and so do I. Because I want not only your body, James. I want your soul.'

James clenched his fists. 'I'll crush you, O!'

'That,' said O with a smile, 'remains to be seen.'

James followed O into another room. Here, kneeling across footstools and cushions, masked but otherwise naked women patiently offered their arses and their vaginas to any man who passed by. James stared, fascinated by the bizarre sight of so many upturned rumps and beckoning cunts. Behind the black masks he caught glimpses of fluttering eyelashes and mischievous smiles.

O took his arm and led him into a bedroom. They stopped beside the four-poster bed that dominated the room. On the bed, hidden behind curtains, a couple were making love. The moans of the woman and the grunts of the man were clearly audible. James made to move away, but O caught his wrist, and made him stop and listen. 'Do you understand this?' she asked him.

James appeared bored; although it seemed to him that

he recognised the voice of the woman who was moaning with delight on the bed. 'So what's the big deal? People fucking, that's all.'

'But don't you think,' O said, 'that these two people, in their daily routine, use civilised language? A vocabulary of thousands of words. And here, in the sexual act, they are reduced to almost nothing: yes, more, no, again, whore, cunt, fuck me — '

'That's enough!' James said.

'No,' O replied, 'it's nothing like enough. You have to see this through to the very end. Otherwise you will not be convinced.'

She pulled back one of the curtains. On her knees and elbows, her back hollowed, her head covered with pillows, Sally Pembroke was being fucked by Karl. She let out a groan as he withdrew his engorged prick from her vagina, and groaned again as he inserted it centimetre by centimetre into her anus. With great deliberation, Karl pushed his hands under her body to play with her large and heavy breasts. He cupped them in his palms; he pulled them to the sides of her ribcage and then thrust into her, pushing her against the sheet and flattening her breasts; his fingers found her nipples, pinching and twisting them until they glowed angrily. Then, resting the weight of his body on her back, he started to slap her breasts with all his strength, one side at a time, pushing into her arse in time with the blows. And all the time James could hear the words that his wife was murmuring; the words that O had just listed: come on, harder, yes, no, please . . . The few syllables of ecstasy.

James controlled his anger. This incident told him nothing new: Botterweg's photographs had been eloquent enough, and the dimension of sound added very little to them. 'So what?' he said to O in an icy voice.

'This should give you pause for thought, James. Another man — a gigolo, a man for whom she pays — can drag from

171

your wife the same cries and moans, the same gasps of ecstasy that you do.'

'I repeat: so what?'

'I wanted to demonstrate that a man does not possess a woman just because he fucks her, because he satisfies her. What counts is what happens before and after.'

'Sally is my wife,' James said angrily. 'That's permanent, and it has nothing to do with this interlude.'

'Marriage doesn't mean much, James. Karl could take your wife away from you.'

James burst out laughing. 'That faggot! I'm a better man than he is — before, during, and after.'

'That wasn't the impression I got on the night that you arrived.'

'Let's drop the subject.'

O smiled ironically. 'You're interested in competition only when your dollars can buy you the victory. Other contests threaten your male pride, it seems.'

'Maybe. All I know is that you just played one of your trump cards. You can't use it again. I'll make better use of this situation from now on.'

Infuriatingly, O merely smiled. 'That's very good, James.'

He decided he had to press his advantage. 'So,' he said, 'whose turn is it next? You going to surprise me by showing me my son putting out for your butler Pierre?'

'No,' was all O said.

'That surprised you, huh? It sure did! I know all about that business too.'

O took his arm and led him away from the four-poster, on which Sally and Karl were reaching a crescendo of frenzied activity. 'I don't underestimate you, James,' she said. 'Please return the compliment.'

'OK, so Botterweg cut you in on his scheme. But what are you really after? This burlesque show doesn't get you anywhere with me.'

'On the contrary, James.'

He stared into her green eyes. 'There is nothing for you to win. Nothing that you could possibly want. I know that for sure. I made enquiries.'

'Ginsberg?'

'Yeah, Ginsberg.'

'Ginsberg is a competent fellow,' O said thoughtfully, 'but there are things that elude him.' When James objected, she went on: 'Oh, I don't mean facts and figures. I'm talking about the essential things. According to your principles, you are quite right: I have nothing to gain from you. But I am not subject to your principles; I am not a reasonable person, James.'

The millionaire was at the end of his tether. He found himself up against an opponent who grew more elusive the longer the game went on, and who played according to her own private set of rules.

'You're trying to get at me through my wife and my son,' he stated squarely. 'It won't work. It doesn't implicate me directly.'

'And your daughter?'

'What about my daughter? She's nothing to do with this. I forbid you to talk about her!'

O smiled, and returned the conversation to the misdemeanours of Sally and Larry. 'And what if all that were to be made public?' she asked.

'I'd do everything in my power to cover it up,' James replied. 'And I'd succeed. I'd have to. A scandal would put me in deep shit. I have a moral system to uphold — the morality of the rich and powerful, which says that in private, anything goes, just so long as the press and the public never find out. Our credibility rests on that morality; and our business interests rest on our credibility.' O made no reply. He nudged her. 'Mighty fine speech, wasn't it?' he said. 'But we can agree on it, at least.'

173

'Not really,' O replied. 'I don't know what morality is.'

They returned to the black-draped room. The men and the women were still there; the scene had hardly changed. The dark-skinned girl was kneeling on an armchair, her knees on the upholstered arms of the chair, her wrists tied together at the back of the head-rest, her black curls covering her lowered head and flowing down her arched back. Sir Stephen was standing behind her, lightly slapping her buttocks with one hand while with the other he rummaged amongst the mass of black hair between her thighs.

He stepped back and beckoned to a younger man. 'Finish her off, would you?' he said languidly.

The young man took Sir Stephen's place behind the girl, opened his kimono, and inserted his member into her vulva. The girl flexed her back, and began to tremble as the man began to move back and forth inside her.

James grimaced. 'Me, I'd finish the job myself.'

O led him to the fireplace. 'It's true that most men take pride in their virility,' she explained. 'But not Sir Stephen.'

'Is that a fact?' James said, not without a hint of envy.

O ignored this. 'He has revived a custom from the Regency period of the *ancien regime*,' she went on: 'the *valet d'amour*. During long orgies, a noblemen who was tired, or elderly, or merely bored, would summon a *valet d'amour* to satisfy his lover.'

'Well you sure don't come across that kind of gallantry these days.'

'In Sir Stephen's case it is not so much a question of gallantry. He is prepared to use a woman's body, but when he does so he uses her as if she were a boy.'

'Then he should stick to going with men,' James said decidedly.

'I think not, James. If you fuck a woman, she can forget

174

you. But a woman always remembers a man who has buggered her.'

'Is that another rule?'

'It's simply the truth,' O replied.

Exasperated beyond endurance, James grabbed O by the shoulders, and found himself looking down into the deep green pools of her eyes. He pulled her towards him, pressing her body against the sudden hardness of his desire. She opened her lips and he covered her mouth with his. Their tongues met.

They remained locked together. O turned slightly so that James had his back to the door and was unable to witness the entry of his daughter.

Jane was in chains and otherwise naked except for a hood that covered her hair and concealed her face. Beneath the hood her head was contained within a mask that covered her eyes and ears. She could hear, as if at a great distance, a low murmur of indistinct conversation; but otherwise the only sensations she experienced were the weight of the chains about her wrists and the tug of the leash that was attached to her collar.

She felt the leash slacken. She stood still. She had no idea where she was, or who was present, or what was going to happen next. But she sensed — perhaps she caught a scent of perfume — that O was nearby, and that comforted her. Hands gripped her shoulders, pushing her downwards. She knelt on the carpet and then, without needing the further prods and pushes, she lowered her head to the floor, arched her back, and lifted her hindquarters into the air to await the inevitable sting of the whip.

A few metres away, O held James's head against her neck and looked over his shoulder at his daughter's punishment. James lost himself in O's body, his hands searching under her dress for her arse and her cunt. 'I can assure you, little lady,' he murmured, 'you won't be able to forget me.'

175

O smiled and kissed his ear. 'And you won't forget me, James,' she whispered.

The man who was flogging Jane was warming to his task. He was using a long leather strap, with a wooden handle, that struck the skin with a satisfyingly loud crack but did not leave a permanent weal. Having reddened the whole expanse of her outthrust buttocks, he used his foot to spread her thighs more widely, and he concentrated his blows on the insides of her thighs, the lowest parts of her arse cheeks, and the furrow between her buttocks. At first Jane had been relieved that the pain of each blow was less intense, less fiery than the whip; but now each stroke seemed to build towards a crescendo of agony, and she cried out each time the strap struck home. Her yells and whimpers were lost among the shouts and groans that echoed from all corners of the room.

James had unfastened O's bodice and was sucking one of her nipples. He felt it stiffen against his tongue. His hand roamed between her legs; and at the moment that he introduced his finger into her anus, O lifted her head as if in surprise or delight. At that signal, the man with the strap stopped whipping Jane. He knelt behind her, moulding his body to hers and covering them both with the expansive folds of his tunic. Jane felt a spear of flesh entering her vagina as the hard muscles of the man's stomach pressed against her tender buttocks; and a spasm of pleasure shook her body.

Now O disentangled herself from James's embrace. She pushed his hand away. 'No, James,' she insisted, 'not like that. You will make love to me, but in the way that I choose.' James turned angrily and stared into the fire. 'This way,' he heard O say; and when he turned back he found that O was hugging to herself the body of a young girl. Her green eyes glowed at him above the hood that covered the girl's head. James could see nothing of the girl but her back and her buttocks. He found himself enthralled by the sight of

176

these perfect spheres of flesh, firm and yet soft, criss-crossed with fading whip-marks and blazing as red and hot as the flames of the fire. 'James,' O said, 'I want you to make love to my eyes.'

James hesitated. 'Are you frightened?' O teased him; and she put her hand against the girl's belly, pushing her tormented arse towards him.

James unbuttoned his trousers and pulled out his member, thick and brown and, it seemed to him, already about to explode with desire. O stroked the girl's back. 'Look into my eyes, James,' she said.

He stood behind the girl, not yet touching her, and he stared into O's emerald gaze. O was gently caressing the girl, making her ready, bringing her to the brink of pleasure; and soon she said to James: 'Now – take her!'

He seized the girl's hips, separated her buttocks, and grunted as her entered her back passage. The girl flinched from the sudden assault, but O held her tightly, and toyed with her sex, and she relaxed again. 'My eyes, James,' O reminded. 'Look into my eyes.'

James started to thrust into the girl's arse. He was sure he had never before experienced such intense pleasure. O's eyes, which seemed to be darkening as he stared into them, had hypnotised him. O moaned weakly, and let her head fall back slightly; her lips opened, her eyes became unfocused. These signs of ecstasy were too much for James. In a delirium he felt a fountain of bliss rising within him, wild and unstoppable. As he spurted his rapture into the girl, he sank his teeth into her shoulder, drawing blood and leaving an undisguisable wound.

O supported the girl and, looking over her shoulder, she threw the American millionaire a triumphant smile.

20

Sunshine streamed across the breakfast table. James Pembroke appeared to be in an excellent mood. Sally, on the other hand, had dark rings under her eyes and was daydreaming over her cup of tea. Larry, dressed in tight white jeans and a red T-shirt, was stuffing himself with honey and jam. Jane, in spite of the heat, was wearing a dress that was buttoned up to the collar.

In an unexpected burst of affection, James took Sally's hand and kissed it. He waved a hand towards the nearby forest and the shimmering blue surface of the pool. 'This is one beautiful day, sweetheart,' he said. 'Let's take a walk in the park.'

Sally withdrew her hand. 'Oh no, honey. I didn't sleep well last night. I need to lie down again for an hour or so.'

James was used to getting his own way. 'Come on,' he insisted, 'just to please me, OK? You ought to make the most of the opportunity. I've pencilled in a whole hour for us to be together.'

'Well I declare,' Sally exclaimed, 'if that isn't just the last word in romance!' But she saw that her husband was frowning, and she relented. 'OK — I'll make the effort. You've got your hour.'

James patted her gently on the back. 'You're a good wife to me,' he said.

'You ever thought otherwise?' Sally asked.

'Not for one moment,' he said, and finished his tea. 'This really is fantastic weather!'

Larry could tell that his mother was feeling put out. He guessed that she had made other plans for the day, and he decided to help out. 'Mom looks real tired,' he said to his father. 'You shouldn't make her come with you if she doesn't want to.'

James's laughter had a hollow ring. 'Well now! There's a dutiful son! I'm real glad you're so concerned about your mother's welfare.' He pointed at his son with his cigar. 'You plan to take her place, I guess? No, I guess not. I bet you're also exhausted after a tiring evening last night.'

Larry stared back at his father. 'Dad, I can assure you I've never felt better.'

'Swell!' James shouted. 'I just love it when my family feels well.'

'You seem to be in good form this morning, too, Dad,' Jane observed.

James seemed not to notice that her voice was weak and cracked. 'I sure am,' he said, rubbing his hands together. 'Business is booming, and here I am sitting with my family.' In a very deliberate voice, he added: 'A true American family: healthy and united.'

Sally felt she had to protest. 'You're going too far, James. We all know that it's your so-called success that makes you happy.'

'Tell me! Tell me about my success, why don't you?'

'We're happy with it if it makes you happy,' Sally said with a wan smile.

'Right!' James grinned. 'So let's be happy!' He offered his cup to Jane, who poured tea into it. 'Business is getting boring, anyway,' he went on. 'I ought to get into something else. Something evangelical, maybe . . . or politics . . . '

'If I were you, Dad,' Jane said, 'I'd skip religion.'

'You're probably right, baby doll,' he said. 'Not enough prestige. I guess I'll stand for the Senate.'

Jane picked up a newspaper from beneath her chair. She passed it to her father. 'I guess you can't have read the papers today,' she said quietly.

James took the paper. Across the front page was the headline:

THE PEMBROKE ORGIES
MILLIONAIRE'S FAMILY IN SEX SCANDAL

James looked at his wife, and then at his children. They had all read the story; they were waiting for his reaction. He crumpled the paper and threw it down the stone steps. He stood up and slammed his fist on the table.

'I don't need to read this shit!' he bellowed; and in a lower voice, he went on: 'I know who is behind this dirt. He's double-crossed me, and he's going to pay for it. Tomorrow the papers will print what I tell them. I've got the money and the power to buy those people. They'll tell it like it is: a healthy and united family, a family whose reputation has been unjustly tarnished — '

He paused to catch his breath. 'A healthy and united family — my ass!' he said dully. 'A faggot, a pervert, and a woman so stupid she falls for the first male whore she meets.'

Larry was keen to demonstrate his new-found confidence. 'You've no right to treat us like this!' he declared.

'You're my family,' James said. 'I'll clean you up whether you like it or not.'

'I feel perfectly clean, James,' Sally said. 'From head to toe. And free, too. I'm through with playing the model wife and mother.' She stood up. 'I'm going.'

James grabbed her arm, digging his nails into her wrist. 'You'll stay here!' he ordered. He released her arm. 'You're all staying here. We have to face this together.'

'Why should we?' Larry said. 'So you can keep on running your businesses? So you can pile up a little more power and money?' He stood next to his mother. 'I'm going too.'

'Is that so?' James said. 'Well, run along then. And don't

180

forget to take Pierre along to brighten up your siestas.' He took a deep breath. 'We have to remain calm about this.'

Jane lit a cigarette. She had seen O's slender figure emerging on to the terrace, and felt reassured. 'We're all calm, Dad,' she said. 'You're the one who's acting kind of crazy.'

'I get it,' James said bitterly. 'you reckon you're right in the head, do you? You let yourself be fucked by dozens of guys, you get yourself whipped — that's all perfectly OK, is it?'

Sally gave her daughter an anxious look. 'What are you talking about?' she said to her husband, 'Are you out of your mind?'

Larry tried to avoid explanations. 'Come on, Mom,' he urged, 'don't hang around here. Jane, let's go.'

Sally trailed after her son. She glanced back towards Jane, who remained seated at the table, serene and still.

'You can clear out, too,' James said to his daughter. 'I don't need you.'

Jane watched the woman with green eyes who was making her way across the terrace. 'O was right all along,' Jane said. 'There's only one person in the whole world that you care about — and that's yourself.'

James grabbed a teaspoon and bent it double it his hand. 'I'll deal with O, too,' he warned, 'in my own time.'

The woman with green eyes was now standing behind his chair. 'Are you looking for me, James?' she said softly.

Jane jumped up and ran to shelter in O's arms. O hugged her.

'Come back here!' James shouted to his daughter. 'Get back here or I'll come and get you!'

O pressed the girl tightly against her body. 'Stop, James!' she commanded, as he stepped forward.

He cursed and extended his hands to seize his daughter. O released Jane and with one movement tore apart the back of the girl's dress. James froze as he saw the whip-marks and bruises on Jane's buttocks, thighs and back. And then he followed O's pointing finger — and he saw the bite on his daughter's shoulder. There was no room for doubt. These were the exact impressions of his own teeth, the bite that he had inflicted at the moment of his climax the previous night.

He couldn't breathe. There was no air. He gave a sort of rattle which expired in the back of his throat. Clutching his chest, he fell to his knees. His hands flailed in the air, failed to find any support, and he tumbled down the stone steps. Hand in hand, O and Jane looked down at him as he struggled in the dirt under the blazing sun. His hands scrabbled in the dust, their spasmodic clutchings growing slower.

The women went away.

21

There is another ending to this story.

O would not have wanted to destroy her opponent. She was sufficiently confident of her victory, from the very first day, to spare him a denouement that he would not be able to survive.

As James was reaching for his daughter, intending to drag her from O's arms, he caught sight of Natalie stepping across the threshold and on to the terrace — and behind her was a blonde girl wearing a dress exactly like Jane's. Natalie remained by the doorway, but the girl advanced across the terrace and stood next to Jane. O left them and came to stand behind James; she placed her hands over his eyes.

He felt O's hands leave his face. He opened his eyes. In front of him were two young women with their backs turned toward him. They were dressed identically; they were the same height, they had hair of the same pale gold. He was unable to tell which of them was his daughter.

'Keep still, James,' O said, 'and watch.' She unfastened the buttons that ran down the backs of both dresses. The girls shrugged off the garments, and stood naked. The backs and buttocks of both girls were criss-crossed with weals; but only one them had a bite-mark on her shoulder.

O nodded to the girl who bore the imprint of James's teeth. She turned round. James released a shuddering sigh as he saw that she was not his daughter.

Then O pulled him towards Jane and insisted that he inspect the red ridges that ran in lines across the cheeks of her backside. 'You see, James,' O said, 'it is all true. But it is not quite as bad as you thought.' James ran his finger gently along one of the angry weals. He felt weak and dizzy; but life was returning. He enfolded Jane in his arms and squeezed her for the first time since her childhood.

Natalie and Pierre had already started to bring out the Pembrokes' luggage. The black limousine was gliding along the avenue towards the chateau. James turned round to find that O had gone. He caught sight of the blonde girl, disappearing into the woods behind a line of beeches and poplars. Then he saw O, making her way slowly in the same direction. Sally and Larry joined him on the terrace, and the entire family watched O, who did not once look back.

But before entering the shade of the trees, O lifted her arm and opened her hand. A dark object dropped to the ground. James Pembroke knew what it was: a chessman — the black king — and he knew that he had lost the game.